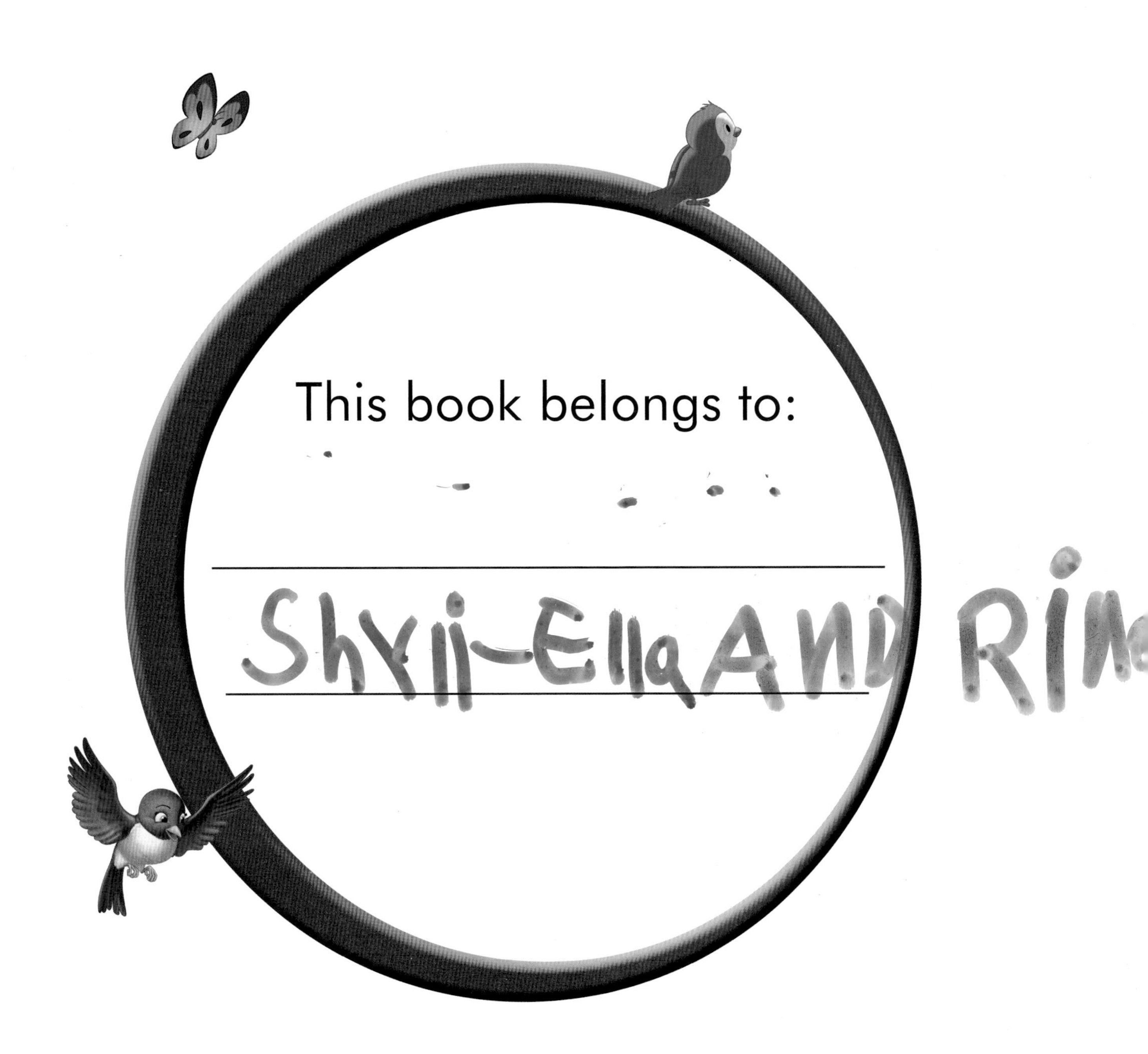
This book belongs to:

Disney
Girls'
Big Book
of Fun

CREDITS
Pages 11–16 | MISS VAN BURLOW'S SECRET
Manuscript: Tea Orsi; Layout and Clean up: Roberto Ronchi;
Ink: Santa Zangari; Paint and graphic illustrations: Giuseppe Fontana
Page 35 | A WONDERFUL DAY
Manuscript: Riccardo Pesce; Layout and Clean up: Paolo Campinoti;
Ink: Michela Frare; Paint and graphic illustrations: Lucio De Giuseppe
Page 36–41 | MERIDA'S WILD RIDE
Copyright © 2013 Disney/Pixar, adapted from the story *Merida's Wild Ride*,
Princess Hearts Classic Storybook #9, written by Susan Amerikaner, illustrated by
Manuela Razzi, Chun Liu, Silvano Scolari, and the Disney Storybook Artists.
Page 66–69 | THE DIFFICULT DELIVERY
Concept and script: Tea Orsi; Layout and cleanup: Sara Storino;
Ink: Santa Zangari; Color: Studio Kawaii
Page 100–105 | A SCARY SLEEPOVER
Manuscript: Tea Orsi; Art: Davide Baldoni; Ink: Francesco Abrignani;
Paint and graphic illustrations: Lucio De Giuseppe
Page 130–133 | AN ALMOST ROMANTIC DATE
Manuscript: Tea Orsi; Layout and clean up: Gianluca Barone;
Ink: Santa Zangari; Color: Studio Kawaii
Page 142–143 | AN ELEGANT SPRINGTIME SURPRISE
Adapted from the story *Cinderella's Spring Adventure*, in *Princess Through the Seasons: Spring*,
written by Cynthia Hands and illustrated by the Disney Storybook Artists.
Page 163–168 | FASHION PASSION
Manuscript: Silvia Gianatti; Art: Stefano De Lellis;
Ink: Santa Zangari; Paint: Angela Capolupo

This edition published by Parragon Books Ltd in 2014
and distributed by

Parragon Inc.
440 Park Avenue South, 13th Floor
New York, NY 10016
www.parragon.com

Visit www.DisneyFairies.com

ISBN 978-1-4723-8501-7

Printed in China

Bath • New York • Cologne • Melbourne • Delhi
Hong Kong • Shenzhen • Singapore • Amsterdam

A New Friend!

What a great day! Brave Merida has joined the Princesses, and they have gathered on the terrace to give her a special welcome!

The new arrival has a proud, strong character, and the other Princesses admire one of her traits in particular. To find out which one, follow the arrow, and in the blanks below, write the letters that appear between each Princess name!
J A S M I N E C A U R O R
L L E A M E R I D A G C A
E E A L L E R E D N I O
B R L E I R A U N A L U M
C _ _ _ _ _ _ _
Ariel
Mulan
Aurora
Answer on page 171

Choose Your Sport!

Imagine you're in the Winter Woods. What sport would you like to try? Choose one of these three pictures and fly over to read your profile!

SKATING

The sport for you is twirling on a frozen lake as gracefully as a butterfly! Just like Periwinkle, you're creative and elegant in everything you do!

WALKING
As lively and full of life as Gliss, you love long walks, even in the snow! All you need is a pair of snowshoes . . . and some company, naturally!
TOBOGGANING
As brave and curious as Tinker Bell, you're always ready to try out new activities. Just be sure to take care of your wings!

Staff Salute!

Meet two of Minnie and Daisy's favorite faculty members from Mouston School.

Welcome to Mouston! I'm **Timber Van Arm**, school principal. I'm originally from the wide-open spaces of Montana, so I naturally **love the great outdoors**. I always try to encourage students to develop an appreciation for the beauty of nature!

More on Mr. Van Arm

Personality:
Tolerant, jovial, enlightened

Best asset:
Wilderness skills

Favorite quote:
"Almost any problem can be solved with a nice walk in the woods!"

Mouston School

Minnie, Daisy, and their friends attend **Mouston School**, a red brick building surrounded by trees and a wide lawn. There's also a garden where students like to chat with friends between classes.

Hello! I'm **Aretha Van Burlow**. I'm the art teacher at Mouston School, and **I love my job**! My students are incredibly innovative and unique—it's fun to encourage and inspire them. I never cease to be impressed by their creative projects!

More on Miss Van Burlow

Personality:
Open, helpful, brilliant

Best asset:
Enthusiasm

Favorite quote:
"Art comes from the heart, not the brain!"

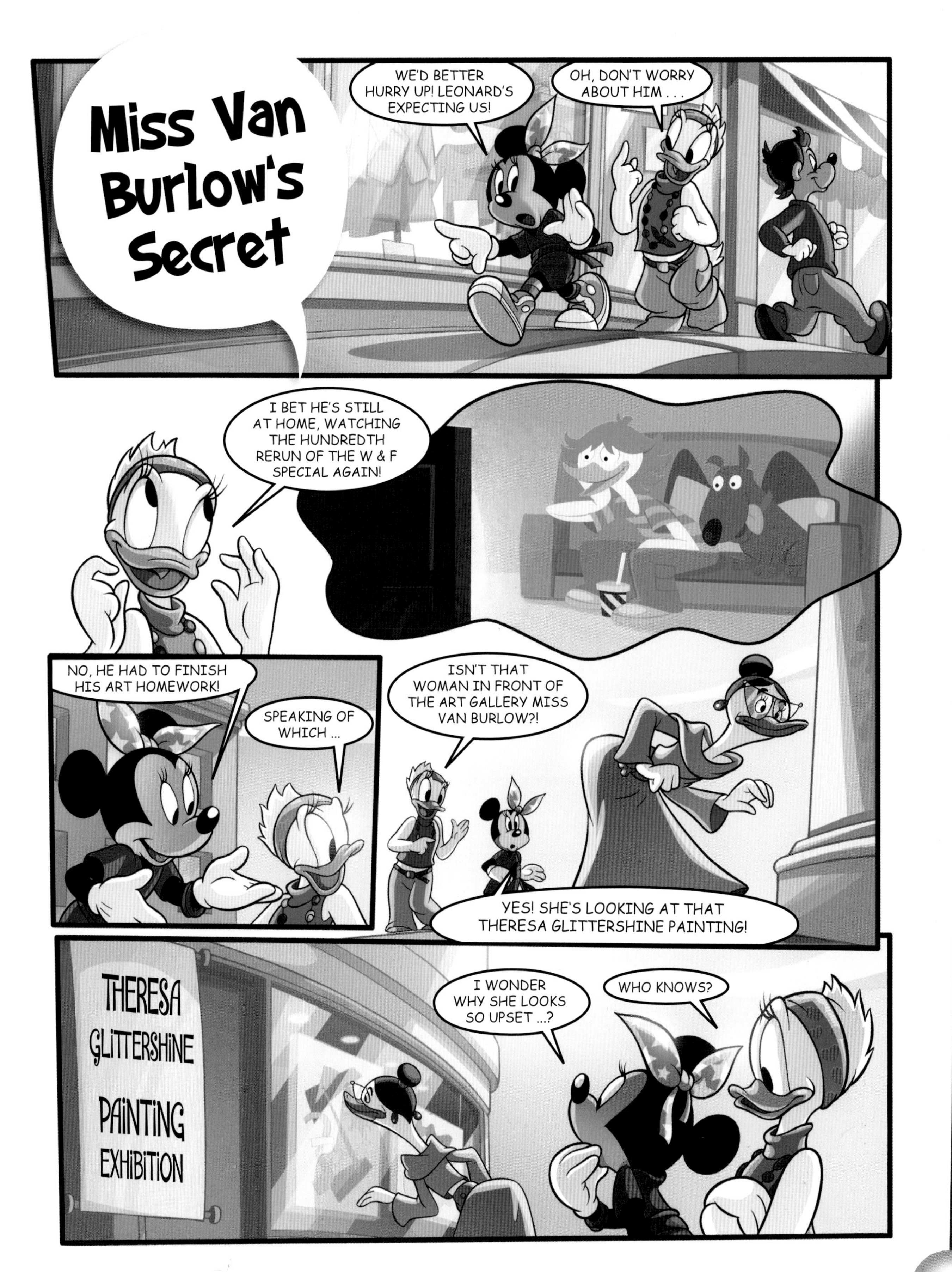

Miss Van Burlow's Secret
WE'D BETTER HURRY UP! LEONARD'S EXPECTING US!
OH, DON'T WORRY ABOUT HIM . . .
I BET HE'S STILL AT HOME, WATCHING THE HUNDREDTH RERUN OF THE W & F SPECIAL AGAIN!
NO, HE HAD TO FINISH HIS ART HOMEWORK!
SPEAKING OF WHICH ...
ISN'T THAT WOMAN IN FRONT OF THE ART GALLERY MISS VAN BURLOW?!
YES! SHE'S LOOKING AT THAT THERESA GLITTERSHINE PAINTING!
THERESA GLITTERSHINE PAINTING EXHIBITION
I WONDER WHY SHE LOOKS SO UPSET ...?
WHO KNOWS?

WHAT DO YOU THINK HAPPENED TO HER?
LET'S GO! I'M SURE IT'S NOTHING TO WORRY ABOUT!
MAYBE SHE DIDN'T LIKE THE EXHIBIT!
COULD BE . . .
INSTEAD . . .
YESTERDAY I SAW HER IN THE SAME EXACT SPOT, AND SHE DIDN'T LOOK HAPPY AT ALL!
REALLY?!
YEAH! SHE WAS PEEKING INTO THE GALLERY AND SEEMED REALLY UNCOMFORTABLE!
WE ALSO HAD THE FEELING SOMETHING STRANGE WAS GOING ON!
SHE GOES BACK TO THE SAME PLACE BUT STAYS OUTSIDE AND LOOKS UPSET!
HMM . . .
MAYBE SHE'S IN LOVE WITH A PAINTING SHE CAN'T HAVE . . .
OR MAYBE SHE DOESN'T LIKE GLITTERSHINE AND WANTS TO TEACH HER A LESSON, BUT SHE CAN'T . . .
OR MAYBE SHE LOVES HER, BUT SHE'S TOO EMBARRASSED TO ASK FOR HER AUTOGRAPH!
SIGH

WELL? WHAT DO YOU THINK?
WAIT! I KNOW WHAT IT IS!
UM . . .
THE TEACHER'S JEALOUS!
GLITTERSHINE IS A FAMOUS PAINTER WHOSE WORKS ARE SHOWN ALL AROUND THE WORLD . . .
BUT MISS VAN BURLOW GAVE UP PAINTING TO BECOME A TEACHER.
SHE MUST REALLY REGRET IT! POOR THING!
YEAH! WE AREN'T EXACTLY IDEAL STUDENTS!
CAPTURE THE SOFTER SHADES WITH YOUR BRUSHSTROKES, AND BLAH BLAH . . .
ZZZ ZZZ
HEY! WHY DON'T WE PUT ON AN EXHIBIT OF MISS VAN BURLOW'S PAINTINGS?!
GREAT IDEA!
WE COULD RENT THE ULTRA MEGA SUPER INTERACTIVE HALL AT THE POSTMODERN ART MUSEUM!
I'VE GOT A SIMPLER IDEA . . .

LATER . . .
OF COURSE YOU CAN HOLD MISS VAN BURLOW'S EXHIBIT IN THE ASSEMBLY HALL!
GREAT!
GULP!
NATURALLY, YOU KIDS WILL BRING THE PAINTINGS HERE!
OF COURSE! SIGH . . .
NOW ALL WE HAVE TO DO IS TELL MISS VAN BURLOW!
JUST IMAGINE HER REACTION!
RUN ALONG! THERE'S NO TIME TO LOSE!
AND SO . . .
HOW SWEET, KIDS! WHAT GAVE YOU THE IDEA?
WELL, WE SAW YOU AT THE ART GALLERY. YOU WERE UPSET, SO . . .

UPSET?!
YEAH . . . I MEAN . . . YOU SURE DIDN'T LOOK HAPPY!
WELL, ACTUALLY, I WAS BORED TO TEARS!
?!
MY FAULT! ARETHA WAS WAITING FOR ME, BUT I WAS TALKING, AND THERE WERE SO MANY PEOPLE, AND TIME JUST FLEW, AND BLAH, BLAH, BLAH . . .
MEET MY DEAR FRIEND, THERESA GLITTERSHINE!
GULP!
AS YOU CAN TELL, SHE'S A LITTLE BIT TALKATIVE.
YEAH . . .
NOT ONCE BUT TWICE I WAITED FOR HER FOR HOURS, BUT SHE KEPT ON CHATTING. I EVEN WENT OUTSIDE!
NOW I GET IT!
AND WE THOUGHT YOU WERE REGRETTING NOT BECOMING A PAINTER!
NO, MY DEAR! I LOVE MY JOB!
IT'S TRUE! ARETHA LOVES TEACHING! IT'S HER LIFE, HER DREAM, HER PASSION, HER MOST—
I THINK THEY UNDERSTAND, THERESA!

IT WAS KIND OF YOU, BUT I'M NOT INTERESTED IN EXHIBITING MY OLD PAINTINGS!
WHAT A SHAME! THE PRINCIPAL WAS SO EXCITED ABOUT IT!
THEN WE COULD HOLD A DIFFERENT EXHIBIT. . .
YOU KIDS CAN PAINT THE PICTURES! THAT WAY, THE PRINCIPAL WILL SEE HOW TALENTED MY STUDENTS ARE!
A WONDERFUL IDEA!
?!
WE'LL WORK ALL WEEKEND LONG AND I'LL SUPERVISE!
WONDERFUL! IT'LL BE AN AUTHENTIC ARTISTIC WORKSHOP!
BLAH, BLAH, BLAH . . .
WELL THEN, I'LL GO CALL EVERYONE!
CAN WE EXHIBIT A DIGITAL PAINTING?
NEXT TIME YOU HAVE AN IDEA, REMIND ME TO RUN AWAY IN TIME!
THE END

Keyed Up!

Unlock It!

The missing part of each sentence below is a number. Find the combination to the lock below by choosing the correct numbers and writing them in the boxes.

A There are ___ players on a basketball team.
- 13
- 5
- 8

D IX is the Roman numeral for ___.
- 4
- 3
- 9

B Snow White and the ___ Dwarfs.
- 5
- 10
- 7

E A duet is performed by ___ singers.
- 2
- 4
- 3

C Sextuplets are ___ siblings.
- 5
- 6
- 8

A B C D E

Key Search

Each of the keys below has an exact match, except one. Find the key with no duplicate!

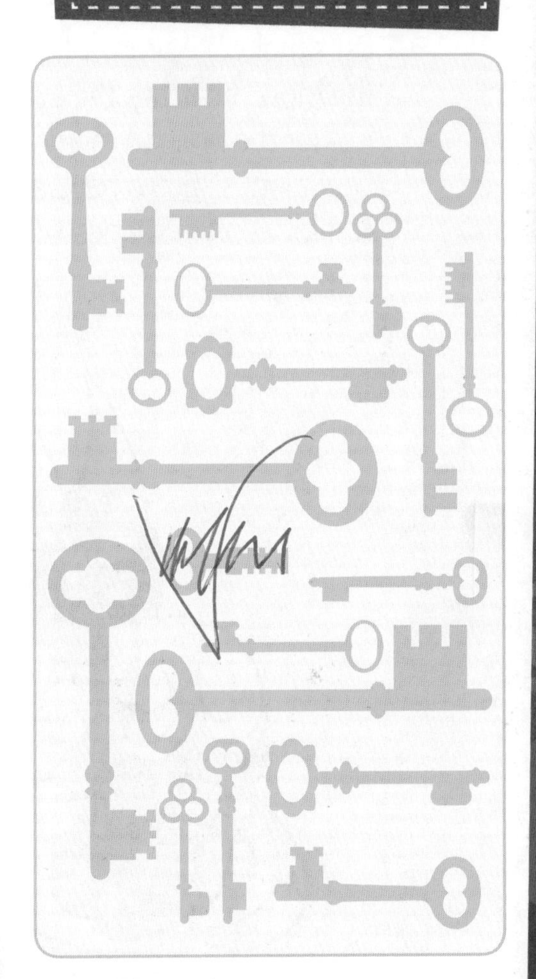

Answers on page 171

Your BFF Brand

Design your own logo with your BFF, and wear your symbol everywhere!

A logo is a symbol representing a company or organization— every major company has one. Because it's easier for people to identify a visual mark rather than words, a logo has to be stylish yet simple. The simpler the design, the more it catches the eye, and the easier it is for the brain to memorize the logo. Great logos should have a perfect combination of shapes, colors, and letters.

Why not create your own personal logo? You and your BFF can have fun designing one to represent your friendship. You might even put your logo on your favorite T-shirt or cap, just like a major clothing label. Imagine wearing your own brand to school!

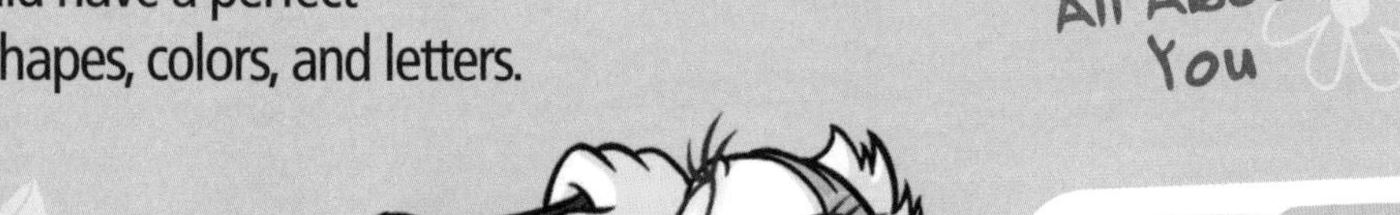

Wear It!

WHY NOT TRY DRAWING OR TRACING YOUR LOGO WITH MARKERS?

You'll Need:

Cardboard

Color Fabric Markers

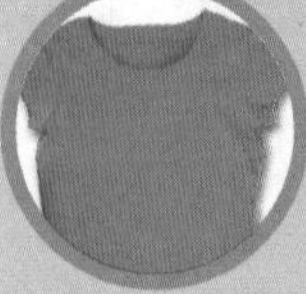

T-Shirt

Scissors

Design It!

The first thing to do is decide what your logo will look like!

- **Get together with your BFF and think about ideas.** What will your brand represent? What do you want your logo to say?

- **Do you want an object or animal to represent your brand?** If so, choose something that says "you." If you're all about nature, for example, a tree might be a good symbol.

- **Sketch out some ideas for your logo,** such as different ways of combining your name or initials with your BFF's.

- **Once you and your BFF have a design you both love,** draw a final version in the colors you want. You could also use your computer to create the logo!

DO IT NOW!

1. Draw your logo on cardboard.
2. Cut it out to make a template.
3. Trace the logo using fabric markers.

Tip

Cut out templates work best with simple designs.

Tip

Always ask a parent for help when using scissors!

A Garden in Bloom!

Rosetta and Iridessa are gathering all the fireflies in the Flower Garden. Help the two fairies by finding and counting them all.

Answer on page 171

Tink is
telling her friends
about her latest
adventure. Color
the picture.

Friendship = Surprises!

When BFFs get together, you never know what exciting things might happen!

Dear Minnie and Daisy ...

My BFF is always coming up with off-the-wall, spur-of-the-moment ideas for things we should do.

I like to plan things a little more, so the chaos drives me a little crazy! Am I being too rigid?

from ... *Cautious*

Dear Cautious ...

Planning is a really good thing, but sometimes it's fun to be spontaneous, too! Next time your friend throws out a suggestion that seems a little unusual, **give it a little consideration before saying no** (as long as it's not dangerous, of course). By being brave and trying something new, you might be surprised at how much fun you have!

QUICK CHECK

In Shape

Look up, down, diagonally, forward, and backward in the grid to find the 14 words listed below. Color in all the letters of the word when you find it. When you're done, what shape do you see?

O	B	G	T	O	E	L	A	I
V	P	A	L	Z	D	U	B	G
P	A	I	R	F	A	L	L	Y
I	T	S	U	R	T	G	O	E
H	A	P	P	I	N	E	S	S
D	J	O	Y	E	V	O	L	E
N	Y	F	U	N	N	Y	T	U
I	H	U	D	D	A	F	V	R
U	O	I	J	S	M	T	A	L
R	H	M	I	Q	K	L	S	I

- Pal
- Bud
- Funny
- Add
- Love
- Joy
- Trust
- Go
- Yes
- Happiness
- Friends
- Hip
- Pair
- Ally

That's Cool!

Answer on page 171

Ready, Set, Go!

Go, Rapunzel! She's determined to skip from stone to stone and reach Flynn on the other shore of the pond. Trace over all the stones without lifting your pencil, and remember—you can't turn back!

Answers on page 171

On Max's Trail

Ariel is looking for Max, but where could he be? She sees paw prints in the sand—so to find him, she just needs to follow them. Can you help her?

A seagull is watching the scene from above. Which shadow matches the seagull exactly?

Answers on page 171

One Per Season!

Match the ministers of the seasons with the right close-ups!

Answers on page 171

Sweet As Sugar

Have you heard of the sugar glider? Here are some interesting facts!

Glider Facts

- **The name "sugar glider"** refers to their diet (they feed on sweet nectar) and the flap of skin between their front and back feet that allows them to glide through the trees.
- **A sugar glider is a small marsupial.** Their babies live in a pouch, like a kangaroo.
- Sugar gliders can live for **12–14 years.**
- **When they get scared**, gliders make a funny fussing sound called crabbing.
- **Gliders are very social.** Without companionship with other gliders, they can become very sad.

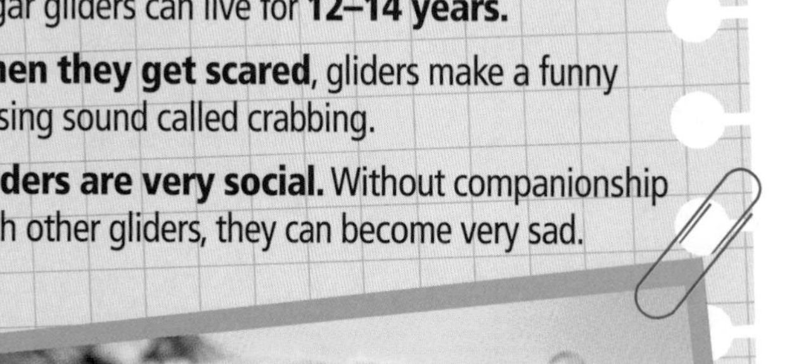

Glide On!

Help the sugar glider find his way through the maze to get to the tree below!

START HERE

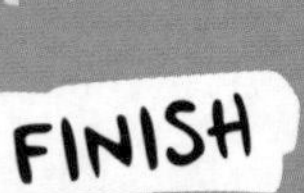

Answer on page 171

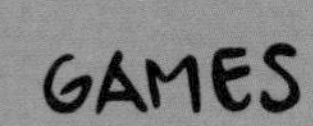

Closet Competition

Pick Up the Pieces

A game for you and your BFF. From your collections below, find the triangles that fit correctly into the empty squares in each section of the closet.

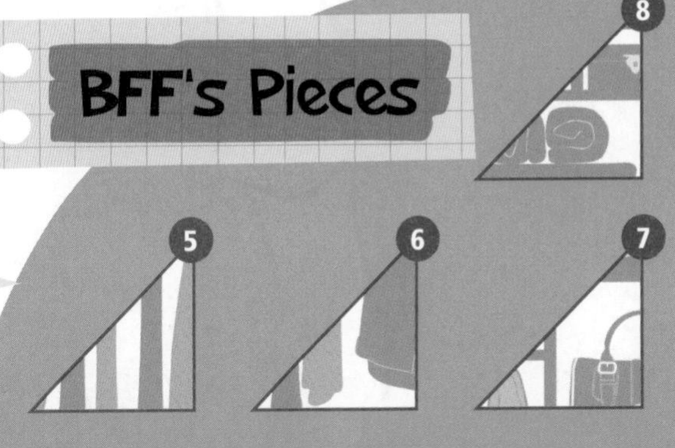

Answers on page 171

A Giant Leap!

John Smith is jumping over the waterfall with Pocahontas. She knows where they can dive safely. Color them in to complete this scene.

Loving Rescue

Naveen went to the river for a stroll, but he's not back yet. He's in danger, but luckily, Tiana springs into action and rescues him. Put these scenes in the right order to find out what happens!

Answer on page 171

The Right Path

Help the little owl find its way over to the Winter Woods.

Answer on page 171

Queen Clarion

The wise ruler of Pixie Hollow, Queen Clarion believes in order and harmony.

Queen Clarion is caring and understanding, but she's also known for making strict rules. For example, long ago, a warm fairy and a winter sparrowman fell in love and crossed the border between seasons to be together. An accident befell them, so Queen Clarion forbade fairies ever to cross the border again.

Who were the two lovebirds? Queen Clarion herself and Lord Milori, who broke one of his wings—an injury for which there is no cure!

Help Queen Clarion reach Lord Milori. Which path should she follow?

Answer on page 171

Great Glasses!

Shine as bright as the sun with stylish shades that flatter your face!

1

ROUND FACE
Offset the fullness in your face with wide **rectangular** frames. Avoid round frames.

2

HEART-SHAPED FACE
If your face is wide at the top and narrow at the chin, **round or cat's-eye shades** look great.

3

SQUARE FACE
Choose oversize or wrap shades for oblong faces, **round or oval** for square faces. These aviator glasses work on either.

4

OVAL FACE
With your balanced forehead and jawline, **any sunglass shape** works on your face—lucky you!

A Wonderful Day

THE END

Merida's Wild Ride

It was a soggy afternoon, and Merida was reading from an old book of Highland tales.

"Look, right there," Merida said. "Magical horses. That one there is called a kelpie. It's a water horse."

Angus snorted. He wanted nothing to do with magic, especially after their last encounter!

The raindrops slowed and the clouds scattered. "Come, lad," said Merida to Angus. "The sun's breaking through. Let's go for a ride." They galloped across the bridge and down the hill.

Just as they reached the woods, a flash of gray caught Merida's eyes. "What was that?"

Angus didn't want to follow—whatever it was. But Merida guided him to a clearing. In it stood a magnificent gray horse. Its coat shimmered. Its mane was like fine silk.

Merida approached, but suddenly, Angus blocked her path. "Angus," she called, "don't be jealous, lad! This horse must be lost. We need to help him—make sure he's safe."

Merida talked to the gray horse, and it responded with a soft whinny.

Merida swung onto the gray horse's back. She didn't have a bridle, but she knew she could guide him with her hands wrapped in his mane. The horse bolted, but Merida wasn't frightened. She had been around horses all of her life.

Merida tried to calm the horse, but he ran on.

They were headed toward a large loch—a deep, dangerous lake. Why did it seem as if her hands were stuck to the horse's mane?

The horse brushed against a tree and trapped rainwater fell down on Merida. Effortlessly, one of her hands came free.

Just ahead, a bridle hung from a tree. Merida stretched to reach it as they passed, but it was just beyond her fingertips. "Angus, help! The bridle!" she called.

Merida could only hope that her friend had heard her cry. There was a cliff ahead, between them and the loch.

He'll stop before we get to it, Merida thought. *Won't he?*

But the horse raced on faster than ever. It seemed as though he'd be impossible to stop!

Merida tugged and pulled on the horse's mane. Nothing worked. She even tried to slide off his side. But she couldn't move.

Suddenly, Angus rushed in front and steered them down a path, away from the cliff's edge. Merida saw the bridle Angus carried. Angus tossed it.

Merida caught it and slipped it over the horse's head.

At last, they reached the shore of the loch. The horse finally slowed to a stop. Merida was no longer stuck. She jumped off.

The stallion stood quietly. Merida looked in his eyes for an answer to what had caused the wild ride. Then she removed the bridle.

The horse's head moved softly before he galloped down the misty shoreline. Merida frowned as she watched him. Was he really racing into the water, or was it the fog playing tricks on her eyes?

Back at the stable, Merida looked at the book she had been reading. She found the legend of the kelpie . . .

"Once a bridle is put on a kelpie, the water horse will do your bidding."

She looked up at Angus. Was it possible? Had she been riding a kelpie?

The End

Beloved Acorns!

Gliss really loves acorns, but so do the other fairies, and animals do, too. Let's find out why!

All-Purpose

While Gliss thinks acorns make flitterific presents, the other fairies find them really handy!

For example, Fawn often wears an acorn "cap" as a real hat, while garden fairies use them as paint buckets, and tinker fairies turn them into wheels for their carts.

A Question of Taste

Lots of woodland animals like acorns, too. They think they're delicious!

On the other hand, these nuts taste really unpleasant to humans. It's a real shame, since acorns are packed with vitamins!

A Special Present

As if by magic, a little acorn can grow into one of the world's mightiest trees—the oak, which in plant language means strength and power. And so, acorns are symbols of good luck and long life.

Do what the fairies do, and give an acorn to your friends!

A little squirrel broke this acorn into two pieces. Which is the right missing piece?

Answer on page 171

Art Smart

Learn more about the many ways you can express your artistic talent.

Everyone is creative in some way, whether through music, words, or even math. If you have a flair for the visual arts, there are many ways you can let it shine. Explore some of the options on these pages, and find the art that best fits your skills and interests.

Art of Friendship!

So Nice!

Art is constantly evolving. Explore your creativity—it may take you somewhere totally new!

Your Art

Art can be found everywhere around us. Don't believe it? Take a look at the list on the right. Check your interests and skills, and find which art form suits you best!

- Cooking … Food styling
- Working with your hands … Pottery-making
- Working with technology … Computer graphics
- Creating stories … Book illustration
- Dressing up … Fashion design

Painting. When you say "art," most people think of paintings because they're one of the most well-known forms of art.

Experiment with different paints—oils, watercolors, acrylics—to find which you enjoy working with most.

Comics Art. Whether in comic books, comic strips, or graphic novels, comics art is extremely popular and has gained respect in the art world.

Try sketching your own character, then create an adventure for him or her and draw it in comics panels.

Graffiti. What began as writings or drawings sketched or spray-painted in public places, has become a real art form, also called street art.

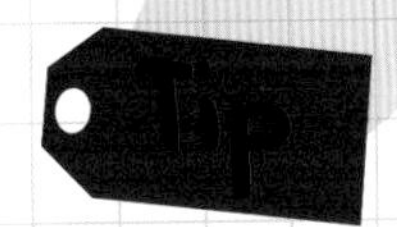

Practice graffiti-style art first using markers on paper. You shouldn't paint on a wall or other surface without permission!

Animation. This means displaying a sequence of images to create the illusion of movement. Animation artwork is used to produce a cartoon.

Practice! Draw a ball in a different position on each page of a notebook. Flip pages to see the ball bounce!

Photography. Photographic art is taking pictures to share your visions and emotions with others.

Composition is very important in art photography. Try to capture interesting patterns or details in your photos.

PLAY

Mulan's Test

Mulan is an adventurous girl who also likes to dream. Which side of her character is strongest in you? Choose your favorite pictures, then trace the arrows that lead to them until you reach either the pink or lilac dots. You'll find out if you are more an adventurous girl or a dreamer.

START

= Adventurous

= Dreamer

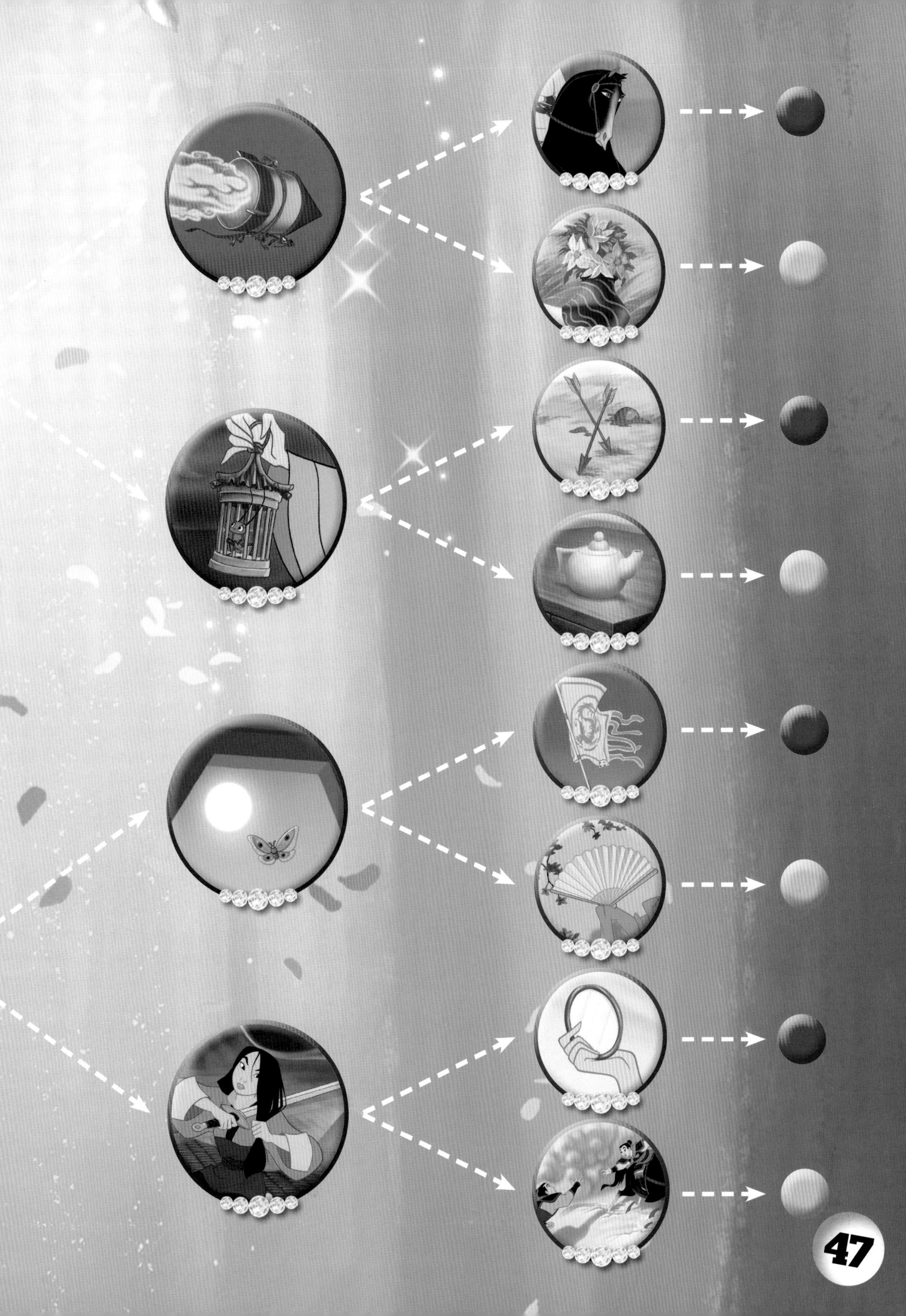

Vidia

Vidia's a super-speedy, fast-flying fairy who loves a challenge!

She lives at the edge of Spring Valley in a sour-plum tree, but she's always first in line to join a fast-flying race.

Vidia brags that she's the fastest fairy in the Hollow. She certainly has great talent when it comes to raising the wind and breezes, but she also has a rather "prickly" personality. Still, if a friend is in trouble, Vidia's always ready to fly off to help!

Look at these objects and circle the symbol of Vidia's talent!

Answer on page 171

A Magical Meeting

Find the shadow that's identical to the picture of Tinker Bell and Periwinkle, then circle it!

Answer on page 171

True Devotion

What would you do for your BFF? This quiz will show you!

A Friend Indeed!

1. You planned to go to your BFF's house, but you're invited to a party on the same night. You:

- **A** Tell your BFF you can't come over.
- **B** Forget the party, you made a commitment!
- **C** Bring your BFF to the party!

2. Your BFF wants to watch her crush play soccer, but you don't want to go. You:

- **A** Pretend you're sick and can't go.
- **B** Try to convince your BFF to stay home with you.
- **C** Go and try to have a good time.

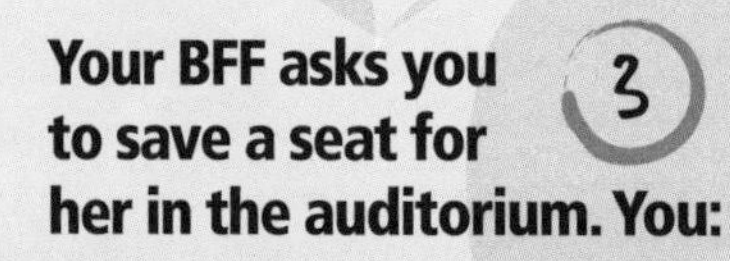

3. Your BFF asks you to save a seat for her in the auditorium. You:

- **A** Accidentally forget about it.
- **B** Take the best seat yourself and save the next one for her.
- **C** Save the best seat for your BFF.

4. You and your BFF both love the same shirt, but there's only one. You:

- **A** Talk her into letting you have it.
- **B** Suggest you each take turns wearing it.
- **C** Let your friend have it—you can always find another shirt!

Your Score

Give yourself one point for each A, two points for each B, and three points for each C. Color one heart charm for each point below, and see where you fall on the necklace scale.

NOT SO DEVOTED — **SOMEWHAT RELIABLE** — **VERY DEVOTED**

Scientific Solutions

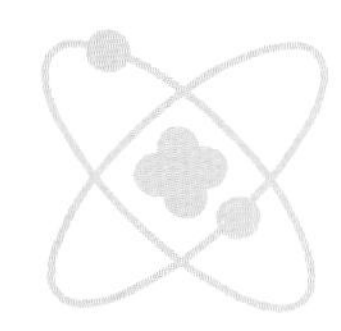

Molecular Mayhem

Look at the three molecules on the right, then find their exact matches in the slide below. Each one appears only once!

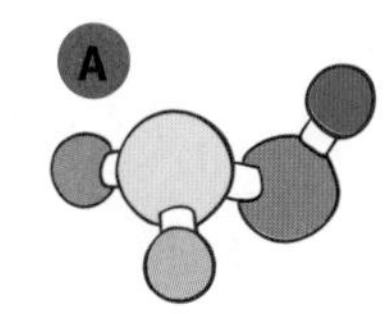

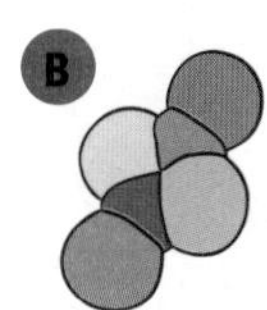

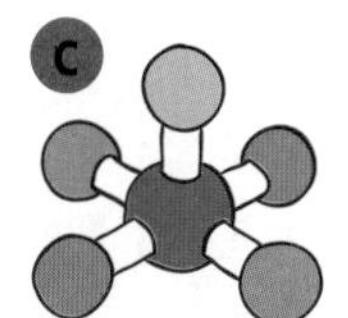

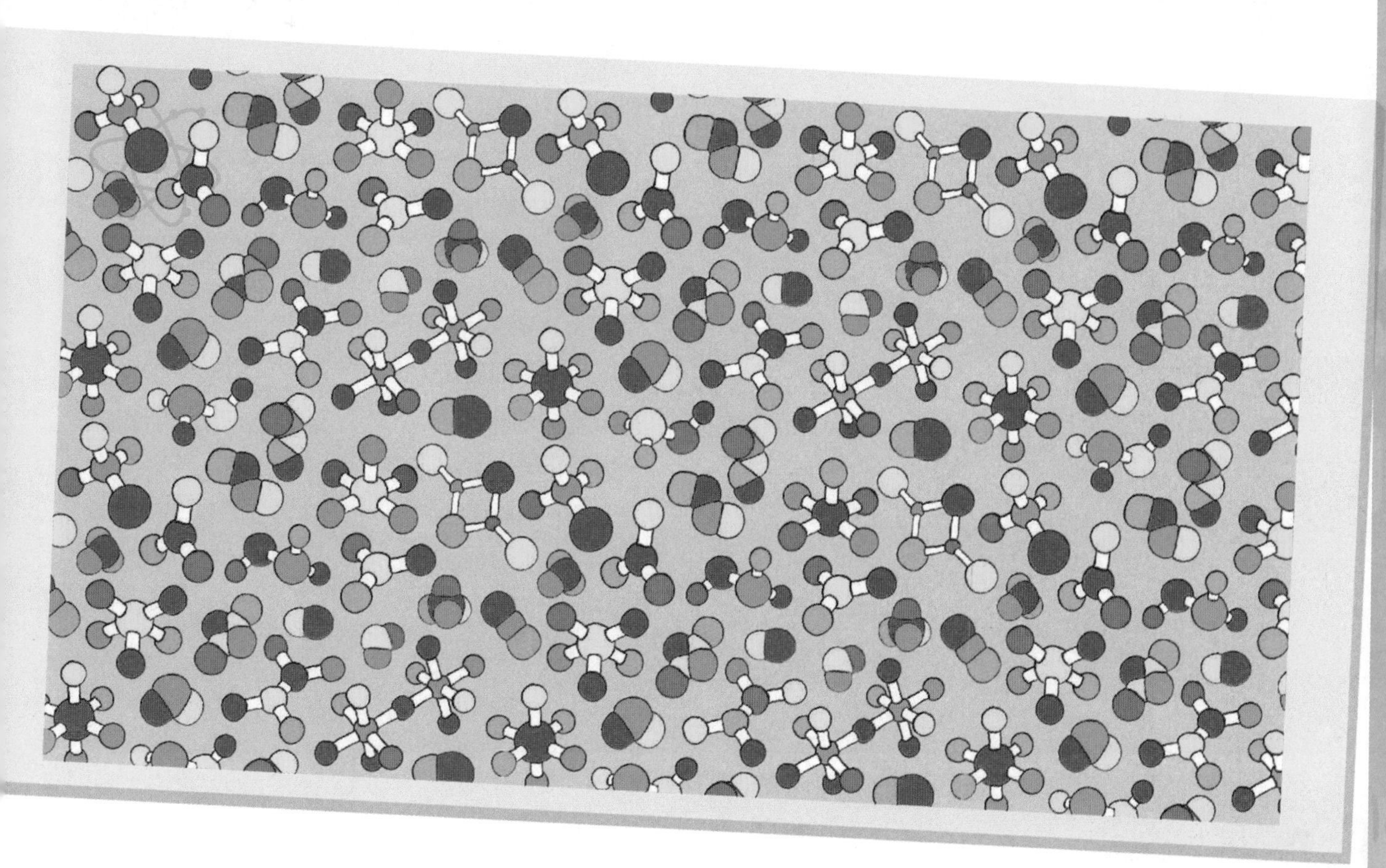

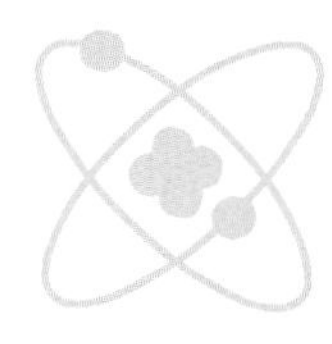

Answer on page 171

In the Forest

Belle certainly is brave, and so are her friends! Without losing hope, they stood up to the wolf in the forest! Look at these two scenes and spot the four differences in the second one to see how everything turned out.

Make a check here for each difference you find.

What is a baby dog called? To find out, cross out every letter A. Then write the remaining letters in the blanks, as they appear from left to right.

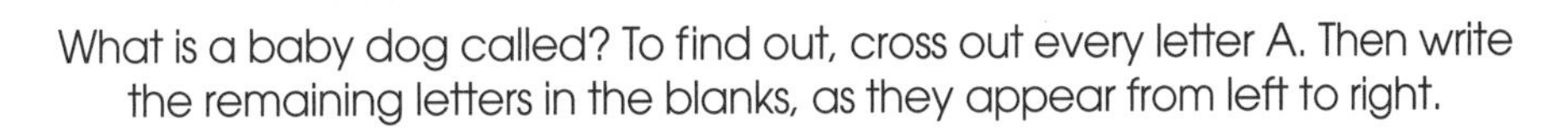

P ___ ___ ___ ___

This little dog sure is brave, and Belle rewards him with a new collar and tag. Trace the number that describes this little champion and color it in!

Answers on page 171

Color the
picture so Tink
can fly over to the
Winter Woods and
go on a flitterific
new adventure!

QUIZ

What's Your Style?

Take this quiz to find out which type of style suits you best!

Your favorite color is:

- A Blue
- B Red or pink
- C Different every day

You spend your free time:

- A Attending club meetings
- B Shopping
- C Playing sports or writing songs

Your favorite part of school is:

- A Socializing with your friends
- B Dressy school dances
- C Gym or art class

Your go-to shoes are:

- A Loafers
- B Cute flats
- C Funky boots or sneakers

You couldn't live without your:

- A Plaid skirt
- B Lip gloss
- C Favorite thrift shop

Your friends think you are:

- A Traditional
- B Fashionable
- C Unusual

You'd love to spend an evening:

- A Playing games with friends
- B At a party with your crush
- C Finding cool music at an old record store

Just My Style!

Mostly As:

PREPPY

You have a **traditional, tailored style** —you like well-fitting clothes with classic, simple lines.

Mostly Bs:

ROMANTIC

You love staying on top of the latest trends, and your style is **feminine** and **full of fun**!

Mostly Cs:

INDIE

Your edgy style is all your own—you're a maverick who wears what you want, rather than what everyone else is wearing!

Spread the Word!

Quick, a friend needs help! Trace the path from Snow White to the moles, following the animal sequence shown in the box at the bottom of the page, to reach the log to rescue the bear cub.

Answers on page 172

So Many Books!

Draw the three kinds of books in the grid so each one appears only once in each row and each column.

Answer on page 172

Fly with Tinker Bell to discover the Book Nook.
Tink is happy because she's finally found the wingology book she was looking for. Color the picture!

Fashion Safari

Shopping Daze Maze!

Find your way through the maze below, collecting all four accessories at different stores on the way to the finish line.

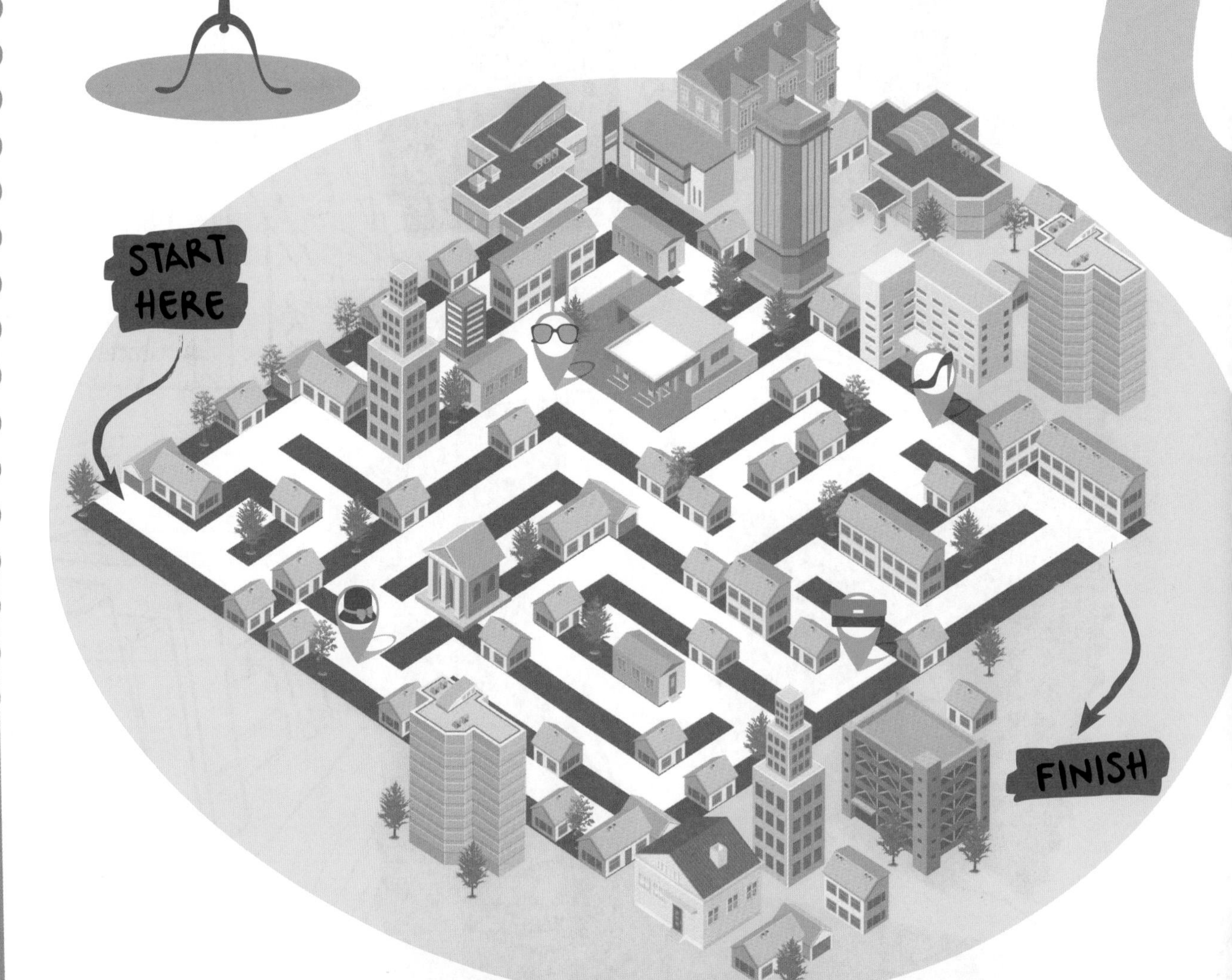

Answer on page 172

Gym Dandy!

Which artistic gymnastics event is for you?

In artistic gymnastics, athletes perform leaps, jumps, and other moves in short routines on the balance beam, vault, other equipment, and the floor. **Find out which event is perfect for you with this quiz!**

Great Routine!

1 People are amazed at my:

- **A** Soaring leaps
- **B** Splits
- **C** High-speed handsprings

2 I can be described as:

- **A** Musical
- **B** Flexible
- **C** Strong

3 I have super-strong:

- **A** Legs
- **B** Core muscles
- **C** Shoulders

4 Athletically, my best asset is:

- **A** Grace
- **B** Balance
- **C** Power

Go for the Gold!

Mostly **A**s:

Audiences would love your dance routines!

Mostly **B**s:

You could do eye-popping moves on a thin rail without falling.

Mostly **C**s:

You'd be amazing launching high and doing all those flips!

Stamp It Out

Create your own stamps to leave personalized great marks!

Stamps are an easy way to make cool designs on cards, wrapping paper, or anywhere you want to add a touch of creativity. And they're easy to make! **Follow these steps to create your own personalized stamps—and have fun with them!**

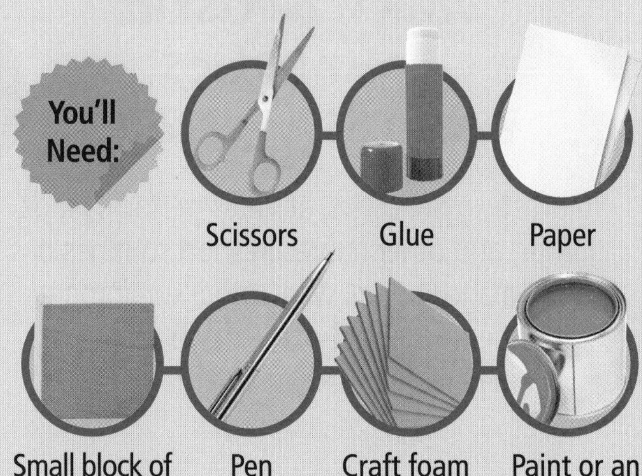

Always ask a parent for help when using a knife or sharp scissors!

Make Your Own Stamps

1. Draw a design on the foam or sponge, and carefully cut it out.

2. Glue the foam shape onto the block of wood and let it dry.

3. To use the stamp, dab it onto an ink pad or a saucer of paint—or you can use a brush to apply the paint to the stamp.

4. Lightly press the stamp onto a piece of scrap paper first, to make sure the stamp works properly.
Now your stamp is ready to create fun designs anywhere!

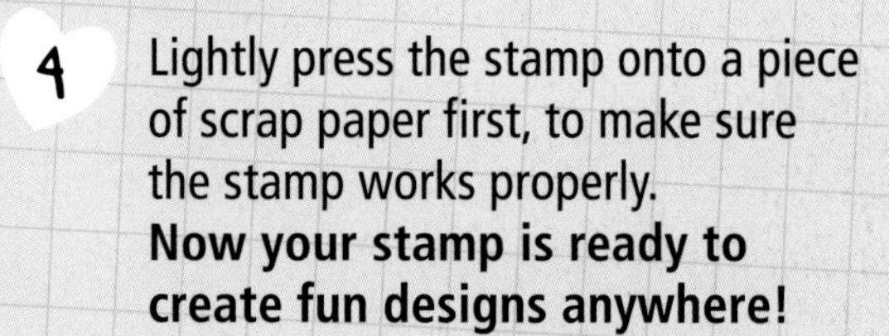

YOUR TURN!

**NOW THAT YOU HAVE YOUR STAMP, USE IT!
MAKE YOUR OWN GREETING CARDS, OR ADD COOL DESIGNS TO YOUR SCRAPBOOKS, NOTEBOOKS . . . YOU NAME IT!
PRACTICE YOUR STAMPING TECHNIQUE HERE:**

The Difficult Delivery

I'D LIKE AN ACORN!
AN ACORN?!
YES, I LOVE THEM! THEY'RE SO CUTE WITH THOSE LITTLE CAPS!
THAT'S ALL THANKS TO US GARDEN FAIRIES, NATURALLY!
AND SO . . .
WAIT HERE! WE'LL FLY RIGHT BACK WITH YOUR ACORN!
WE'LL FIND THE BIGGEST ONE WE CAN!
THANKS!
THE FAIRIES FLY BACK TO AUTUMN FOREST AND . . .
THERE ARE SO MANY TO CHOOSE FROM!
YOU'RE RIGHT!
ALL WE NEED TO DO NOW IS TAKE IT BACK TO GLISS!

MUCH LATER . . .
PANT! IS THIS EXHAUSTING!
UNFORTUNATELY, WE DON'T HAVE ENOUGH PIXIE DUST TO MAKE IT FLY!
WELL, LET'S REST A MOMENT, AT LEAST!
GOOD IDEA, BUTTERCUP!
BUT . . .
CRUNCH
GULP!
I HAVE A BAD FEELING ABOUT THIS . . .
OH NO!
NOW WE HAVE TO GO BACK AND GET ANOTHER ONE.
?!

AND SO . . .
WE'RE ALMOST THERE!
IT WAS TOUGH, BUT SINCE WE DIDN'T STOP, WE DIDN'T RISK . . .

. . . LOSING IT.
PLOFF
GASP!

WHAT NOW? DO WE START ALL OVER AGAIN?
FORGET IT!

I'VE GOT A BETTER IDEA!
SOON . . .
TA-DA! TO MAKE YOUR PRESENT EVEN MORE FUN, WE HID IT IN THE SNOW FOR YOU TO FIND!
HEE, HEE!
WOW!

THE END

The Power of Two

With the strength of friendship, you can make it together!

Dear Minnie and Daisy ...

In gym class this year, I will have a fitness test in which I have to climb a rope as part of my grade. I have never been able to climb a rope—it's really hard! **My BFF says she's confident I can do it**, but I'm afraid I'll fail! Do you have any tips?

from ... *Anxious*

Dear Anxious ...

Your BFF is right—with the right preparation and belief in yourself, you can do it! The key is to practice so you get a little stronger every day, and build your confidence with positive thinking. By the time the test rolls around, with **your supportive BFF** in your corner, you'll conquer that rope!

Dear Minnie and Daisy ...

My BFF is always putting herself down, and I don't know why because she's really cute and cool. What can I do to help her understand how beautiful she really is?

from ... *Confused*

Beatriz and Alex always back each other up!

QUICK CHECK

Tennis Match

Daisy is playing in a tennis tournament, and Minnie is waving a pennant to cheer her on! Among the flip-sided pennants below, find the one with the exact reverse set of colors.

Answer on page 172

Dear Confused . . .

One of the greatest things a friend can do is support her BFF and boost her confidence. Make sure your BFF knows how great you think she is. And be specific—if she has great style, say so. If she's the funniest person you know, tell her! If she knows you believe in her, she'll believe in herself!

A Stroll in the Woods

The Princesses are enjoying a lovely stroll, when suddenly their animal friends stray from them! Follow the threads to see who's accompanying each one!

To find their friends, the Princesses will have to follow their paw prints in the park! Ariel and Snow White found these prints. Who do they belong to?

Answers on page 172

The World Around Us

All the "Juice" of Summer!

They're the tastiest fruits in the Summer Glade. Rosetta thinks they're perfect for breaking the ice and turning on the good cheer!

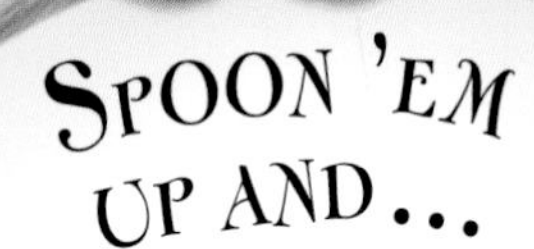

Spoon 'em up and . . .

Ripened at the height of summer, these bunches of brightly colored berries make great juice—sweet and slightly tangy, just right for thirst-quenching drinks.

Whole berries may be used for jellies, fruit salads, and desserts! For a super snack with your friends, crumble a couple of cookies into a cup and add yogurt and jelly. Then chill in the refrigerator, and decorate with fresh fruit.

. . . brush 'em on!

Berries come in lots of colors: red, pink, black, and yellow!

It's not surprising that art-talent fairies are especially fond of berries. They mix different color juices with a pinch of Pixie Dust to paint their masterpieces . . . like the ones they paint on butterfly wings!

Friendly Buds

Currant buds have an intense scent and are used to create perfumes and beauty creams.

The fairies also use this plant to make a syrup that helps them resist chilly gusts (and the heat, too!) when they fly to different seasons.

1

2

Here are two bunches of currants—which has more berries?

Answer on page 172

Sleepytime

Whether you invite one guest or one hundred, planning a pajama party with your BFF is a blast!

Like most things in life, planning a pajama party is more fun with your BFF! Decide whether you'd like to have a sleepover at your house or at hers (make sure to clear it with your parents first). Choose a date on the calendar, draw up a guest list, and you're on your way!

Tip

You and your BFF should split jobs for organizing the party. For example, once you decide what snacks to serve, you could buy some and she could buy others. **Each of you could be in charge of different games or activities.** One could be in charge of serving drinks and the other could be the official DJ.

Party Planner

Use this checklist to make sure everything goes smoothly. Either you or your BFF can check off each task as it's done.

- Get permission from parents.
- Send invitations.
- Plan menu and activities.
- Prepare music playlist, movies, and other entertainment.
- Buy snacks, drinks, extra toiletries, and prizes for games.
- Clean and decorate bedroom.
- Prepare any food to be served.

Get Busy!

Check out these ideas for keeping guests entertained:

- Start a pillow fight.
- Create silly hairstyles.
- Hold a karaoke contest.
- Create a dance routine.
- Play board games.
- Make snacks together.
- Stage a ghost-stories contest.
- Start a juicy-gossip session.

Tip

Have a couple of extra toothbrushes on hand in case guests forget theirs.

Pajama Games

Keep your friends laughing with a purse scavenger hunt! Before the party, you and your BFF make a list of all the things girls keep in their purses or backpacks. At the party, go down your list and have everyone look for the items in their bags. A guest gets one point each time she has an item on the list that no one else has.

Consider these items for your list:

Here's a delightful Tiana story to read.
Replace each picture with the right word!

It was almost Mardi Gras in New Orleans and and wanted to decorate a for the big parade. How exciting! Their friends all joined in to help build a truly splendid one, the most beautiful in the whole city! Everyone had something to do: had learned to sew, and she made a gorgeous ; was ready with his ukulele; and would play his . After days of preparation, everything was ready and had a question for all—

A Parade in New Orleans

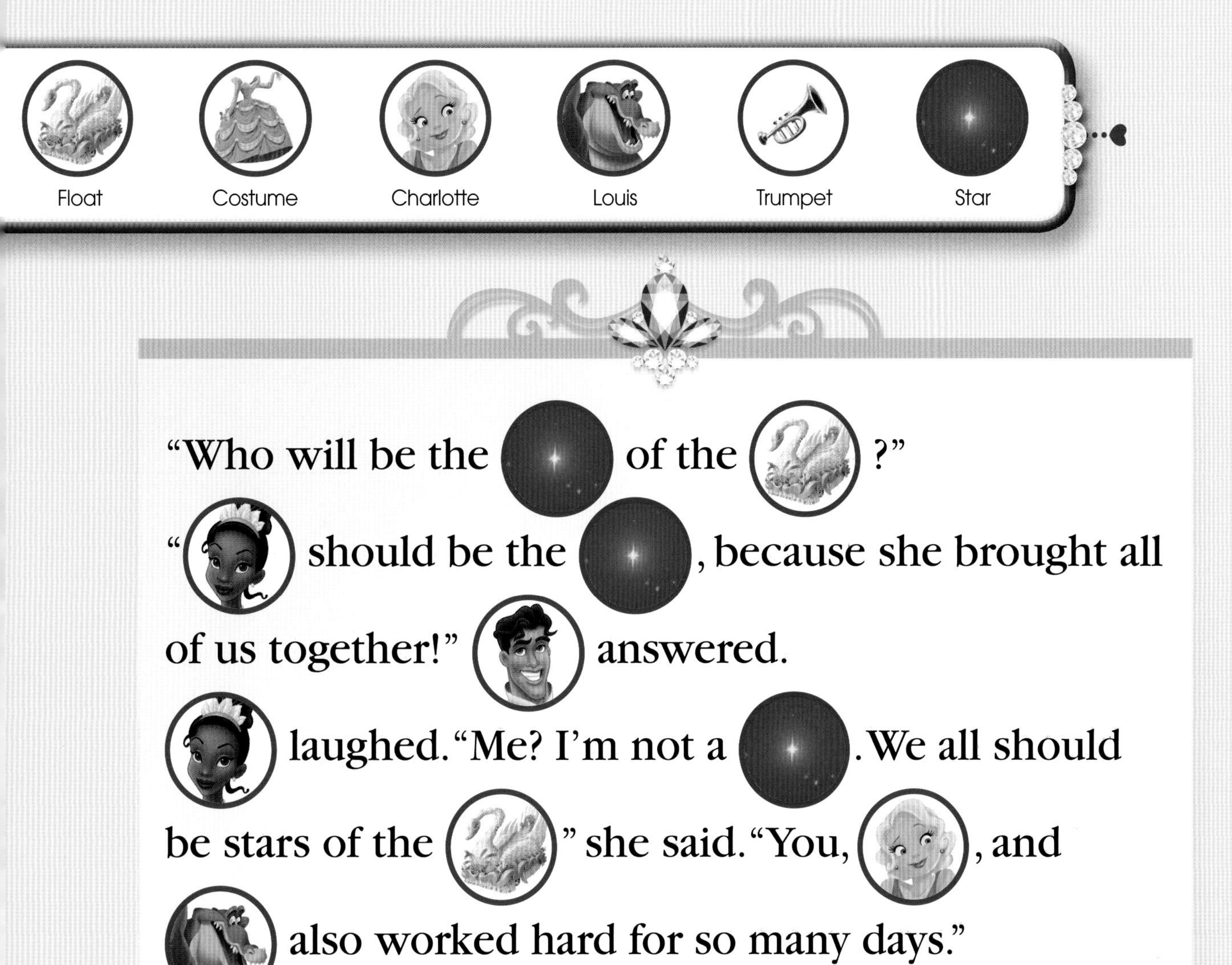

"Who will be the of the ?"

" should be the , because she brought all of us together!" answered.

laughed. "Me? I'm not a . We all should be stars of the " she said. "You, , and also worked hard for so many days."

So on the day of the Mardi Gras parade , , , and rode together on the .

On the streets, people were clapping their hands happily—their was the most admired one!

The Minister of Summer

Free-spirited and jovial, she's a fairy that doesn't go unnoticed!

Like the season she's in charge of, the Minister of Summer is a burst of happiness! She wears a bright summer-blossom dress, and whenever something funny happens, her loud, cheerful laughter echoes all the way to the Winter Woods!

She adores her work, but can't stand rules and discipline. She's a free spirit and often acts more like a doting mother than a Minister. But when the situation gets critical, she takes command and tackles every problem with her incredible energy.

Flower Maze

Rosetta loves to be in her garden—she's even grown a maze out of beautiful flowers! Can you help her find her way out?

Answer on page 172

Friend Files

Find two descriptive words and two pictures below that belong with each character!

Answers on page 172

Matchmaker

Charmed Life

Look closely at the charms on the right and match each figure with the country in which it's known to bring good luck.

- Italy
- India
- U.S.A.
- Japan

1 WISHBONE

3 WELCOMING CAT

2 ELEPHANT

4 CHILI PEPPER

Four-leaf Clover Search

Which one of the numbered four-leaf clovers on the top row comes next in the sequence below?

1 2 3

?

Answers on page 172

Free at Last!

What's that rustling? Rapunzel isn't used to her freedom yet and is afraid of the noises she's unfamiliar with. Look at the ears popping out from this bush. Who's hiding there? Check it below.

Answer on page 172

Maximus and Flynn look more alike than they think! Look at their expressions below and draw lines to link up the matching ones.

Answers on page 172

There's always lots of work to do in Pixie Hollow. Lend a hand by coloring in this scene.

You're in the Movies!

Which movie career is for you? This quiz will give you a clue!

Answer the questions to find the path to your movie career!

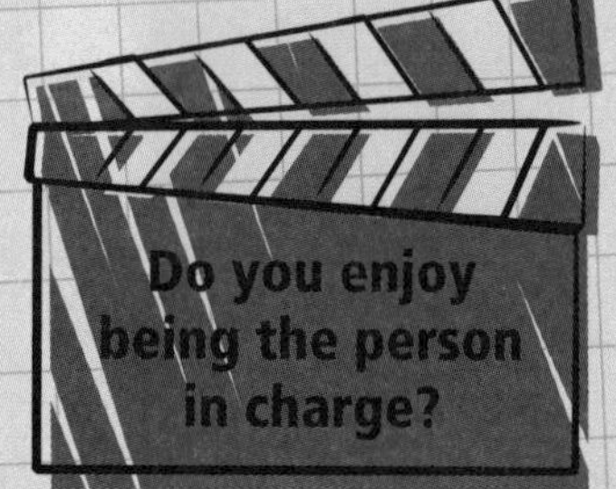

Yes

Set the Scene!

Lights! Camera! Action!

Screen Queen!

Blockbuster!

No
Do you like being in front of the camera?
No
SCREENWRITER
You write the dialogue that makes the characters come to life.
Yes
You're a Star!
ACTOR
Your emotions and actions make audiences fall in love with your character.
Yes
Are you interested in all aspects of movies?
No
Yes
No
DIRECTOR
You're the boss who pulls every part of the movie together.
Take one!
Yes
Do you prefer to focus on one task rather than juggle many?
No
COSTUME DESIGNER
You create the looks that make the characters more believable.
Yes
That's a wrap!

Ocean Friends

The sun is setting and Ariel's friend, a young dolphin, wants to catch up with his family for the night. To help him, circle the sequence of sea creatures on the right—the ones left are his family!

Ariel has lots of friends in the sea. Trace the name of one of her favorites!

DOLPHIN

Answers on page 172

Teamwork!

The fairies are flying over the field of sunflowers, ready to gather the seeds to take to the mainland. Color them in!

Tinker Bell has invented a seed-gatherer to help her friends. Which of these pieces has she used to build the machine?

Answers on page 172

Ancient Astrology

Are you a horse or a dragon? Find your sign in the Chinese zodiac!

Like the familiar Western zodiac, **the Chinese zodiac is a system for identifying personality characteristics** and predicting the future in a person's life based on when the person was born.

A Different Horoscope

There are some major similarities and differences between the Chinese and Western zodiacs. Both have time cycles divided into 12 parts, but in the Chinese zodiac, each part is one year on the Chinese calendar rather than one month. The parts of the Western zodiac are represented by constellations, and the Chinese zodiac is symbolized by **12 animals**.

How It Works

The Chinese zodiac begins with the Year of the Rat, with each following year represented by a different animal. **After 12 years the cycle starts over again** with another Year of the Rat. Your birth date determines which animal symbolizes you.

Late Dates

For each sign below, the most recent years are represented.

Rat

FEB 19, 1996—FEB 6, 1997
FEB 7, 2008—JAN 25, 2009

INTELLIGENT, SENSIBLE, POPULAR, SHY

Dragon

FEB 5, 2000—JAN 23, 2001
JAN 23, 2012—FEB 9, 2013

ENERGETIC, ROMANTIC, AMBITIOUS, IMPATIENT

Monkey

FEB 4, 1992—JAN 22, 1993
JAN 22, 2004—FEB 8, 2005

LIVELY, QUICK-WITTED, SOCIABLE, JEALOUS

What's Your Sign?

Check the list to find out.
Write your sign and your BFF's sign below!

My Sign ....

My BFF's Sign ....

Ox

FEB 7, 1997—JAN 27, 1998
JAN 26, 2009—FEB 13, 2010

HONEST, PATIENT, CAUTIOUS, DISTANT

Tiger

JAN 28, 1998—FEB 15, 1999
FEB 14, 2010—FEB 2, 2011

TOLERANT, ACTIVE, EXPRESSIVE, OVERCONFIDENT

Rabbit

FEB 16, 1999—FEB 4, 2000
FEB 3, 2011—JAN 22, 2012

SENSITIVE, CARING, KIND, STUBBORN

Snake

JAN 24, 2001—FEB 11, 2002
FEB 10, 2013—JAN 30, 2014

UNDERSTANDING, DETERMINED, PASSIONATE

Horse

JAN 27, 1990—FEB 14, 1991
FEB 12, 2002—JAN 31, 2003

CLEVER, KIND, TALENTED

Sheep

FEB 15, 1991—FEB 3, 1992
FEB 1, 2003—JAN 21, 2004

POLITE, WISE, GENTLE, INDECISIVE

Rooster

JAN 23, 1993—FEB 9, 1994
FEB 9, 2005—JAN 28, 2006

COMMUNICATIVE, WARM-HEARTED, BRIGHT, CRITICAL

Dog

FEB 10, 1994—JAN 30, 1995
JAN 29, 2006—FEB 17, 2007

STRAIGHTFORWARD, BRAVE, TRUSTWORTHY, IRRITABLE

Pig

JAN 31, 1995—FEB 18, 1996
FEB 18, 2007—FEB 6, 2008

OPTIMISTIC, LOYAL, IMPULSIVE

Thrilling Tales!

Belle is spending an afternoon in the meadow, with lots of books. What fun, reading about cooking, music, and animals—and enjoying novels! Look at the pictures on the covers and connect the pages below to the books they belong to.

Belle adores reading, and the castle library is full of books! Look at the spines and check off the ones she's chosen to bring with her on this afternoon break.

Answers on page 172

Bird's-eye View

Seen from above, Agrabah is so beautiful. Jasmine is showing Rajah her favorite places! Look at the scene and spot each of the details shown below.

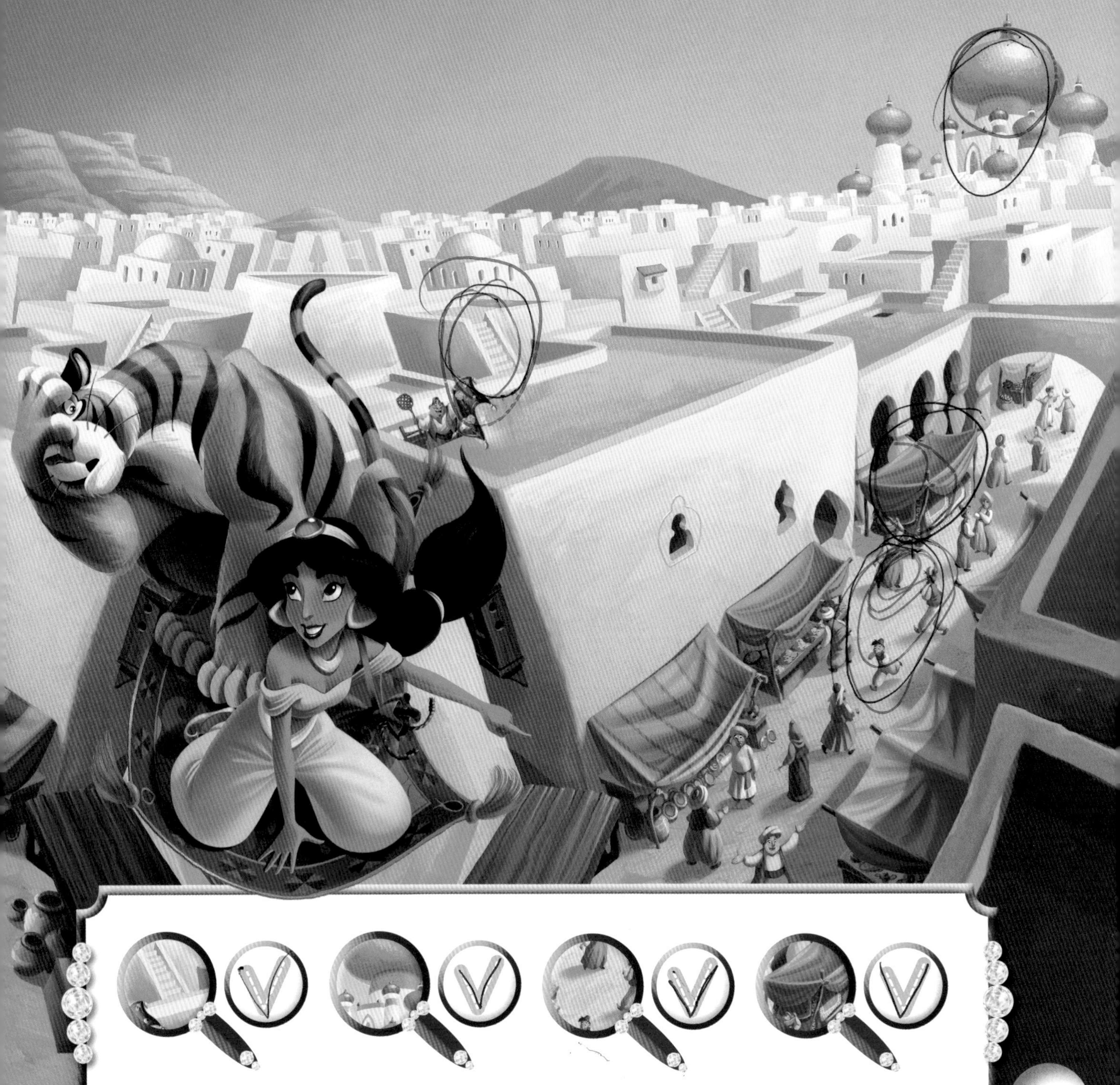

Answers on page 173

The Minister of Spring

Demanding and precise, it's his job to make sure spring starts and ends on time.

Spring means joy, enthusiasm, tenderness ... feelings that don't seem to have much to do with the Minister of this season! An organizational genius, he wants the preparations to bring spring to the mainland to run like clockwork.

Fussy and extra careful in his work, he's also neat and elegant when it comes to his attire and only wears suits custom-made with spring flowers. The Minister of Spring is known for his kindness to plants. Some fairies believe that before he became a Minister he was a garden-talent sparrowman. Who knows?

The Minister of Spring has realized that two flowers have changed places in the sequence here on the right. Can you spot them?

Answers on page 173

Silvermist's Secret

Follow the line that leads from each letter bubble, then write the letter on the correct lily pad to reveal what Silvermist uses to make the pond bubble.

Help this fish find its shadow!

Answers on page 173

A Scary Sleepover
I CAN'T WAIT FOR TONIGHT!
YEAH! I LOVE SCHLUFFIGFUSTEN!

BUT WEREN'T WE GOING TO HAVE A PAJAMA PARTY?

NOW WE JUST NEED TO PICK A MOVIE!
DON'T TELL ME YOU GUYS WANT TO WATCH A THRILLER!

ACTUALLY, WE WERE THINKING OF HORROR!
GULP!
NO! LET'S GET A COMEDY!
BUT SOMEONE IS LURKING IN THE SHADOWS . . .
THIS IS GOING TO BE FUN! HEH, HEH, HEH!
LET'S GO! WE'LL DECIDE AT THE VIDEO STORE!
ANYTHING'S FINE, AS LONG AS IT ISN'T SCARY!

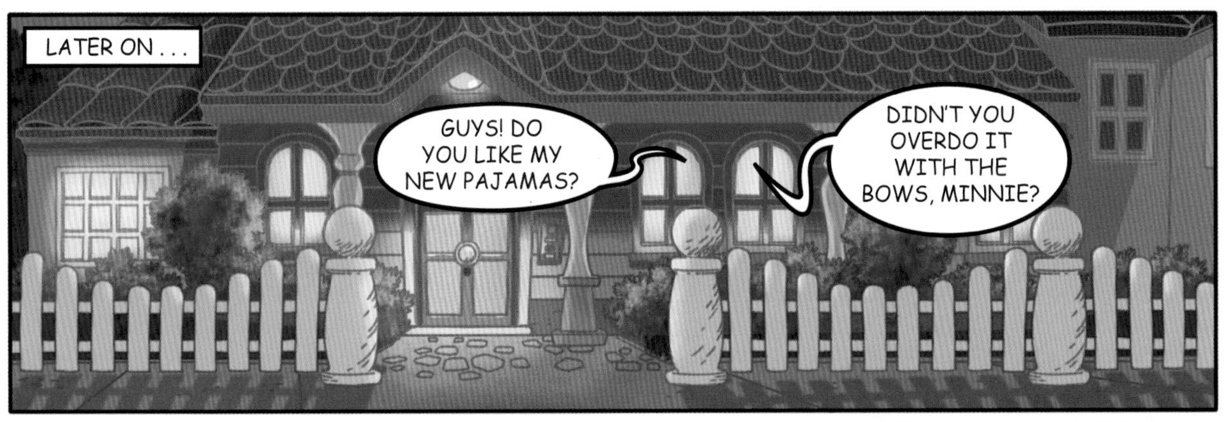
LATER ON . . .
GUYS! DO YOU LIKE MY NEW PAJAMAS?
DIDN'T YOU OVERDO IT WITH THE BOWS, MINNIE?

I THINK THEY'RE REALLY CUTE!
OF COURSE THEY ARE! I WAS JUST KIDDING! LET'S WATCH THE MOVIE!
DVD

BUT . . .
HOWWWLLL
EEEK!

D-DID YOU GUYS HEAR A HUGE HOWL, TOO?
RELAX! THAT MUST BE THE NEIGHBOR'S DOG . . .

I KNOW YOU'RE IN THERE! HEH, HEH, HEH!
GULP!

COME TO THINK OF IT, THE NEIGHBOR'S DOG DOESN'T TALK!
CALM DOWN!
DVD

LET'S GO TAKE A LOOK!
ARE YOU CRAZY?!

MAYBE IT'S A WEREWOLF THAT EATS GIRLS IN PAJAMAS!
DON'T WORRY! I'LL THROW A TUFOFFLEL AT IT!

FINALLY, THE OTHERS CONVINCE MACY TO FOLLOW THEM, AND . . .
MAYBE IT'S THE WIND?
RUSTLE RUSTLE
BUT THERE ISN'T EVEN A BREEZE TONIGHT!

I'D STAY AWAY IF I WERE YOU!
GULP!

LEEEEEAVE BEFORE IT'S TOOOOO LATE!
UM . . . MAYBE WE SHOULD!

LET'S GO INSIDE!
?!
YES! RUN AWAY-AY -AY-AY . . .

DARN IT! THE APP FROZE!
START IT UP AGAIN!

WHAT DO WE DO NOW?
A TUFOFFLEL ISN'T ENOUGH!
DON'T WORRY, GUYS!

I KNOW WHO IS TRYING TO RUIN OUR PARTY!
A WEREWOLF?
A PAJAMA PARTY PHANTOM?

NO! A MINUTE AGO, I HEARD VOICES AND . . . PSST, PSST!
WE SHOULD'VE KNOWN!
LISTEN . . . !

. . .THERE THEY ARE AGAIN!
THEY GOT THE APP WORKING NOW!
HOWWWLLL

GRRR! WE SHOULD TEACH THOSE THREE A LESSON!
I'VE GOT AN IDEA . . .

AND SO . . .
LET'S LEAVE! IT'S TOO DANGEROUS HERE!
WINK

THREE ...

TWO ...

ONE ...

WATER!!!
SPLASH
EEEEK!

AHA! SO THIS IS WHO WANTED TO SCARE US!
ARE YOU CRAZY? YOU JUST ABOUT FLOODED MY TABLET!

AND YOU GUYS ALMOST SCARED US TO DEATH!
WHAT'S THE BIG DEAL? IT WAS ONLY A JOKE!

I JUST WANTED TO TRY OUT THE NEW APP, "SPECTERLIZE YOUR VOICE"!
AND YOU THOUGHT RUINING OUR PARTY WOULD BE A NICE WAY TO DO IT, HMM?

UM ... MORE OR LESS!

WELL, WE'LL LEAVE, SO YOU CAN GET BACK TO YOUR PARTY!
AH-CHOO!
BRR!
I'VE GOT A BETTER IDEA ...

...YOU COULD JOIN US! WE'LL HAVE FUN!
OKAY! I MEAN ... NO! UM ... WE'RE NOT INTERESTED!

C'MON! I'LL LEND YOU SOME PAJAMAS WHILE YOUR CLOTHES DRY OUT!
OH, ALL RIGHT! WE'LL STAY!

AND ...
THIS IS THE MOST RIDICULOUS THING I'VE EVER WORN!
NO! IT LOOKS GREAT ON YOU!

SO, WHERE WERE WE?!
WE WERE ABOUT TO WATCH THE MOVIE!
DVD

A LITTLE LATER ...
I LOVE THIS MOVIE!
WOULD YOU PASS THE POPCORN?
IF I'D KNOWN IT WOULD GO LIKE THIS, I WOULD'VE INVITED THEM RIGHT FROM THE START! HEE, HEE!
ICE

THE END

Pond Mystery

Mommy and Daddy swan have lost their babies! Where could they be? Aurora and the Good Fairies have offered to help find them! See how this adventure ends—choose the right picture and trace the matching arrow.

Answer on page 173

Rainbow Vase!

YOU'LL NEED:

- ★ A medium-size glass food jar
- ★ About 40 colored pencils
- ★ Double-sided tape
- ★ Colored ribbon

Here's a great idea to liven up your room . . . or for a gift to someone special. It's a vase with all the colors of the rainbow!

HELPFUL HINT!

Make sure the jar and the pencils are the right size. The jar must be tall enough to contain your flowers, and the colored pencils must be higher than the jar! Also, since the number of pencils you'll need depends on the diameter of the jar, count them out for a test run before sticking them on.

1

Carefully pick out a color sequence, lining up the pencils on a table. Take inspiration from the rainbow (red, orange, yellow, green, blue, indigo, violet), or change the colors any way you like.

2

Apply double-sided tape around the jar. Stick on the first pencil vertically, with the point on top. Tip: press lightly.

3

Add sequences of colored pencils, lined up next to each other, to cover the jar. Decorate your rainbow vase with a ribbon.

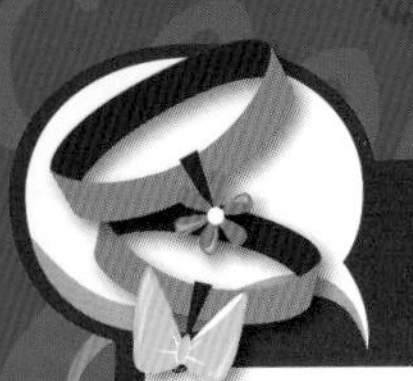

Hop to It!

With preparation and patience on your part, a rabbit can be a great pet!

Rabbits are soft, sweet, and cute—and that's why so many people would love to have one as a pet. But every year thousands of rabbits are left at animal shelters after owners discover that caring for them is too difficult. Make sure you arm yourself with info before you bring this fluffy friend home!

Not for Everyone!

Important things to know about rabbits:

Each one is different.
Some bunnies love to be picked up, cuddled, and played with—but not all rabbits have the same personality. Be aware that some may need some time to get used to human contact.

Prepare for destruction!
A rabbit's teeth never stop growing! These natural chewers will bite into anything, including electrical cords, curtains, and books. So you'll need to bunny-proof your house.

Be a friend.
Rabbits get lonely, and they need companionship. They should never be left in a cage and forgotten.

Bunny Needs

Food and water. Prepare to clean cages and supply fresh hay and water daily, along with pellets and vegetables.

Toys. Keep your bunny busy! A toy can be as simple as a cardboard carton or old towel to chew on.

Cage. House rabbits need cages at least three to four feet long.

Exercise. Don't isolate your pet in a small cage. Rabbits should be allowed to hop around in a rabbit-proofed room or an exercise run for several hours a day.

Bunny Breeds

Match the rabbit to its name!

There are dozens of different breeds of pet rabbits. Can you match the photos below with the name of the breed?

A ☐ **Dutch** Known by white markings on his face and shoulders.

B ☐ **Dwarf Lop** Named for his floppy ears.

C ☐ **English Angora** Has super-fluffy fur.

D ☐ **Lionhead** Known for his royal "mane."

E ☐ **Rex** Has short, dense fur like velvet.

F ☐ **New Zealand Red** Named for his striking color.

Too Cute!

Answers on page 173

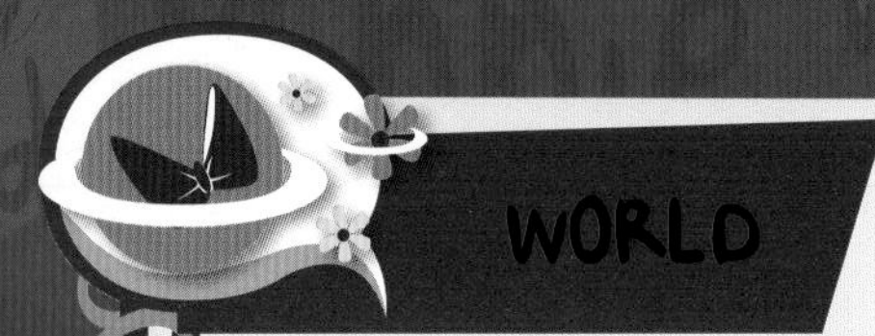

Celebrate Our World!

Earth Day reminds everyone to take care of our environment!

Earth Day was created on April 22, 1970, to bring attention to environmental problems such as air, water, and land pollution. It taught people about actions they could take to help keep the planet clean—such as recycling—and pushed governments to pass environmental protection laws. Now, every year Earth Day is celebrated around the world. It's a time to appreciate the beauty of our planet, learn about new challenges and how to take action, and renew efforts to work toward a clean world.

Your Celebration

JOIN IN THE EARTH DAY SPIRIT! HERE ARE SOME IDEAS:

- **Organize** a community cleanup on Earth Day.
- **Encourage** your friends to stop using plastic water bottles.
- Take shorter showers and **use less water** when brushing your teeth.
- Bring a **reusable** bag when you shop.

QUICK CHECK

A. The **idea** for **Earth Day** came from an environmentalist in Ireland.
○ True ○ False

B. It takes 100 years for a **plastic bag** to decompose.
○ True ○ False

C. The **Amazon rain forest** is sometimes called "Earth's green lung."
○ True ○ False

Answers on page 173

Pets at Play

You know that exercise is good for you, but did you know that it's also good for your pets?

Working out gives you energy, keeps your muscles and joints flexible, helps you live longer, and makes you feel better. It can do the same things for animals.

Plus exercise helps burn off excess energy, so your playful pup is less likely to chew on the sofa. Make sure your pet gets a chance to get up and get moving!

Caged Pets: Bigger animals like rabbits, and large birds like parrots, need time outside their cages. If possible, let your pet out in a safe room to stretch while you are cleaning their cage.

Cats: Cats are designed for short periods of intense activity. Give your kitten plenty of toys that he or she can explore, chase, scratch, and bat around, like paper bags, empty boxes, string, or an old piece of carpet. You'll soon figure out which kind of toy is his or her favorite!

Dogs: A workout for your dog can be just as fun for you! Take him or her for a walk, or just run and play in the backyard—dogs love to play chase and fetch. The amount of exercise needed varies depending on the breed, but most dogs should get 30 to 60 minutes of activity each day.

Night Spell

It's a beautiful night, perfect for making a wish come true, and the Fairy Godmother is casting an incredible spell to help Cinderella. Spot the four changes she's just made with a twirl of her magic wand!

The Fairy Godmother's spell ends at midnight! Check off the clock that strikes the right time.

Answers on page 173

Fairy Facts

A Library of Flittering Fun!

The books in the Book Nook are filled with Fairy Wisdom! It's also one of the quietest places in Pixie Hollow, as long as Tinker Bell's not around . . .

Books in Motion!

Some books have special shapes . . . and special effects! For instance, the book on wingology has pages shaped like wings and, when opened, can even fly!

The pages of some books are sometimes munched upon by bookworms! Luckily, the scribe-talent fairies quickly rewrite the missing pages!

The Roots of Wisdom!

The Book Nook is nestled among the roots of the Pixie Dust Tree. Its walls are lined with shelves containing thousands of books—from *The History of Pixie Hollow* to *101 Uses for Pixie Dust*, which Terence helped write!

Tome, the librarian, knows each book by heart and where to find it. Some fairies even suspect he sleeps in the library!

Secret Code

Tinker Bell wants to know who wrote the book about fairy wings. Use the special code to find out!

e h k p r t

___ ___ ___   ___ ___ ___ ___ ___ ___

Answer on page 173

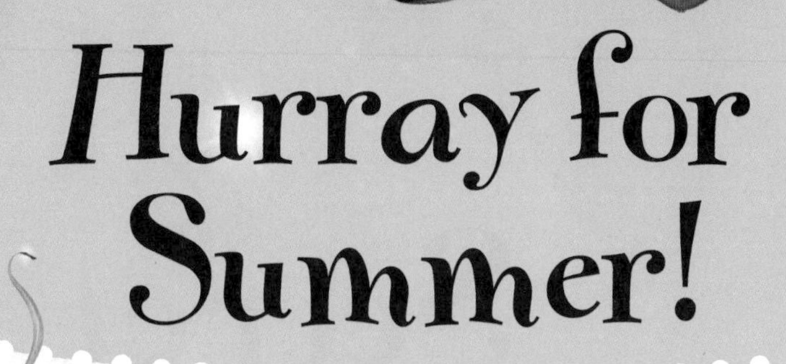

Hurray for Summer!

Silvermist loves decorating spiderwebs with dew drops, so that they sparkle and shine in the sunlight. Put her webs into the right order, starting with the web that has the least number of dewdrops on it, and end with the web with the most!

Write the correct sequence here:

____

Answer on page 173

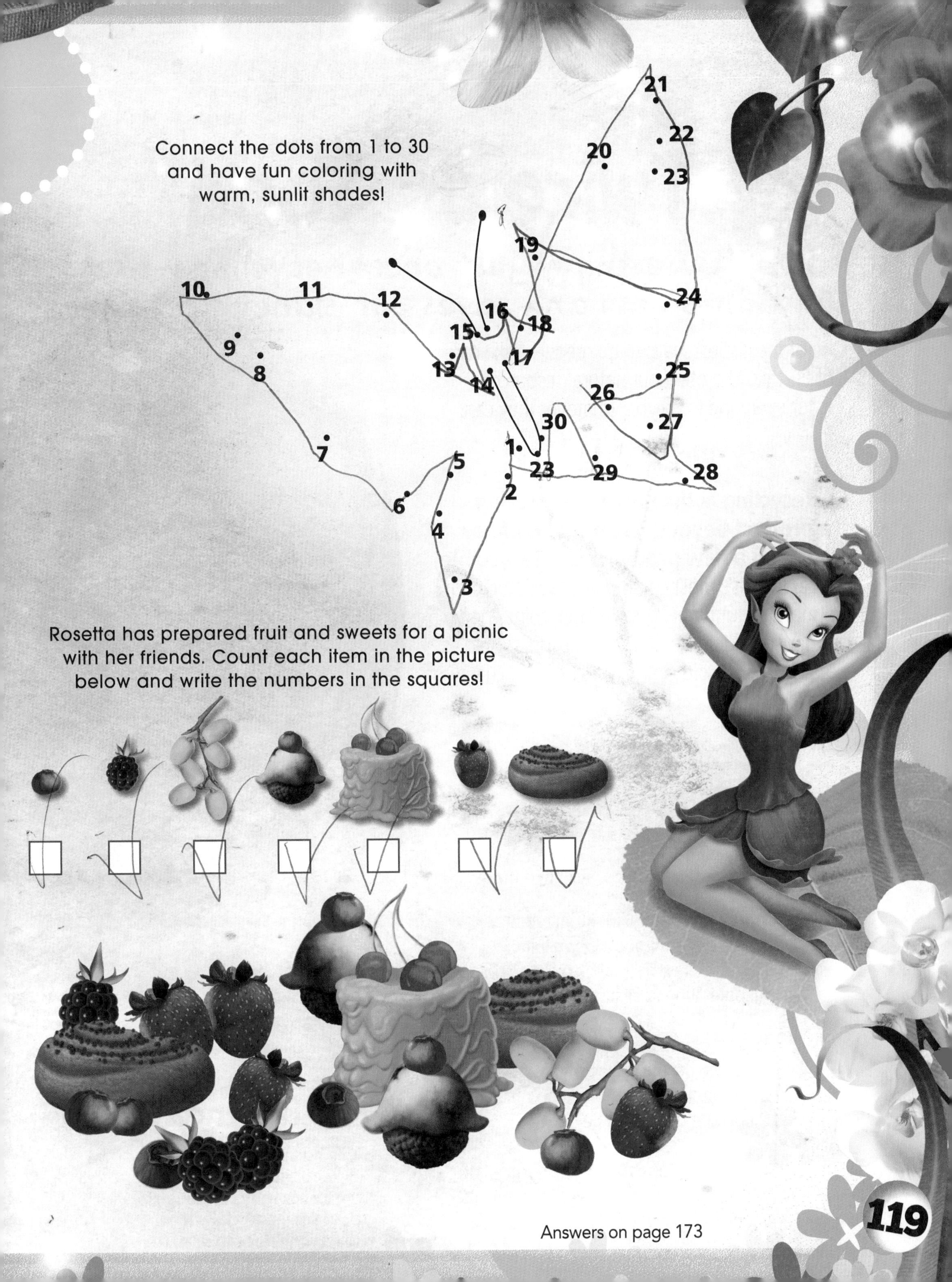

Answers on page 173

Twice as Good

Don't use things just once! Recycling makes old things new and saves our planet's resources!

One of the easiest ways to go green—take care of Earth and protect our natural resources—is for everyone to recycle whatever they can.

What It Is

Recycling is the process of reusing a product beyond its intended life or producing a new product from recyclable materials. It's most commonly associated with re-manufacturing old goods and turning them into new products, but it also can be as simple as passing on your old clothes to a friend or charity.

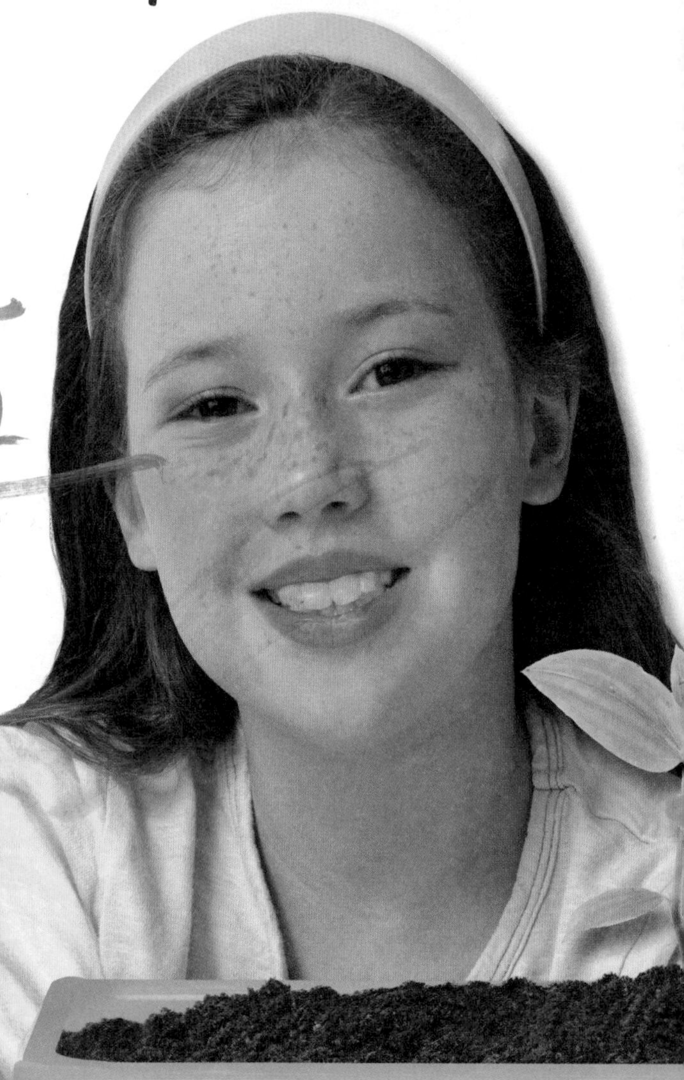

Why Recycle?

Recycling is good for the Earth (and for us) in lots of ways, including:

- **It saves energy.** Manufacturers don't have to produce something new from raw natural resources, so manufacturing consumes less energy.
- **It preserves our resources.** There are more people on the planet every day using our resources. If we don't preserve them, one day they'll be gone.
- **It reduces landfills.** If we're recycling, we're throwing away less, which means we need fewer landfills.

Make a Difference

Can one person really help keep the whole planet green just by recycling? Yes—especially if everyone does their part!

QUICK CHECK

What's New?

Match the plastic bottle, newspaper, and aluminum can below with the two numbered items that can be made by recycling these materials.

1

2

3

4

5

6

A Plastic Bottle

B Newspaper

C Aluminum Can

Homework!

Take a look around your house and make a list below of things you could recycle!

- - - - - - - - - - - - - - - - - - - -

- - - - - - - - - - - - - - - - - - - -

- - - - - - - - - - - - - - - - - - - -

If you throw one aluminum can into a landfill, it will still be a can 500 years from now! **But recycle it and it can be back on the store shelf as a new can in just 60 days.** Recycling just one plastic bottle can save enough energy to power a 60-watt light bulb for six hours. Now imagine if everyone in the world recycled!

Answers on page 173

Royal Hairstyles

Each princess has chosen a different look for her hair. Some are into accessories, others go for updos, and there are those that let it flow! Check them all out!

Aurora, Snow White, and Jasmine are wearing delightful accessories in their hair! Check the ones that are not in the picture.

Answers on page 173

Rapunzel's hair
is so long and
beautiful! Have fun
coloring it in with
three different
shades of yellow!
Some princesses
prefer elegant
updos.
Check off
the ones who
wear this style.

Fairy Quiz

Quit or Try Again?

As Rosetta and Sled know, things don't always go the way you want them to. But they keep trying and refuse to give up! How do you deal with situations that go sour?

Answer these questions to see which fairy you're most like.

1. **Before leaving for vacation, a friend asks you to take care of her plant. Now the leaves are drying up. What do you do?**
   - Buy another one that looks just like it.
   - Take even better care of it.
2. **In the pool you want to show your friends a super dive off the board, but you end up doing a belly flop! Now what?**
   - Give it another try.
   - Oh, well . . . at least you got everyone's attention!
3. **You give your friend a plush toy for her birthday. What do you do when you find out someone else has given her the same one?**
   - You give her two different color bows for her "twins!"
   - Pretend it's no big deal.
4. **At the gym there's an exercise you can't manage to do. So . . .**
   - You keep practicing.
   - You apologize and don't do it.
5. **A friend replies grumpily to something you've said. What do you do?**
   - Walk off in a huff.
   - Try to understand what she's thinking.
6. **You've almost finished your latest work of art, but a drop of paint suddenly drips where it shouldn't have. Now what?**
   - Throw away the painting.
   - Wait till the drop dries and try to fix it.

MOSTLY

Tinker Bell

You're as determined as your tinker-talent fairy friend! Even when things go wrong, you never give up. On the contrary! Your spunk doubles and your wings flutter like crazy!

Tink's Tip: Use your talent to help someone in need!

EQUAL AND

Rosetta

You're sweet and kind, just like Rosetta. But you also can be stubborn when you have to be! So what if you blow it—you can smile and try again if it's worth the effort.

Rosetta's Tip: If it's important to you, go all out!

MOSTLY

Vidia

You love winning—that's Vidia all over. Your determination is unflagging, you're a high-flying ace of the skies, but when things go haywire and you get tripped up, you'd rather forget the whole thing.

Vidia's Tip: Giving it a second try isn't so embarrassing really, is it?

Star Friendship

Does give-and-take come naturally in your friendship, or do you have to work hard to compromise? **This compatibility horoscope may show you why!**

Work It Out Together!

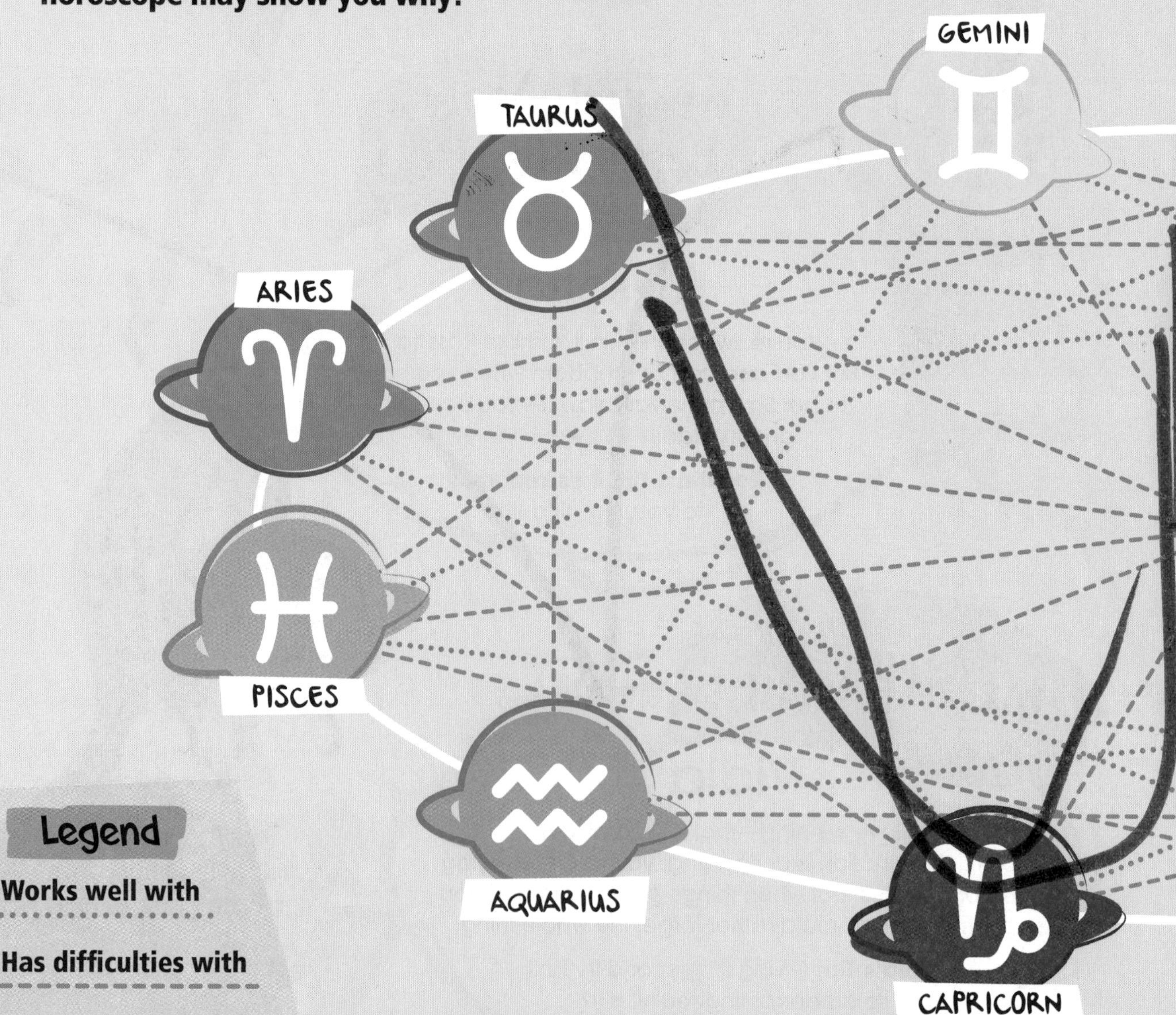

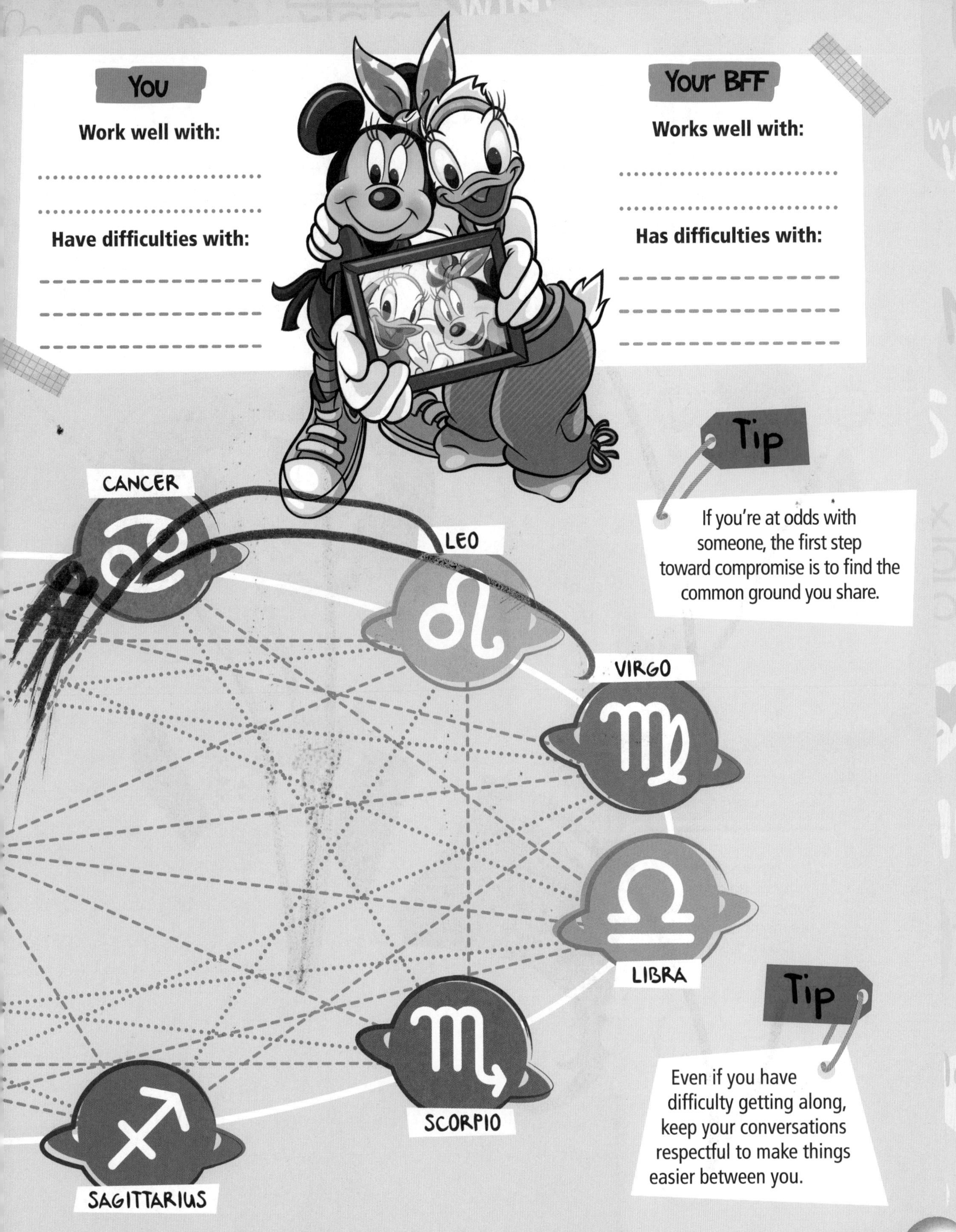

Tip

If you're at odds with someone, the first step toward compromise is to find the common ground you share.

Tip

Even if you have difficulty getting along, keep your conversations respectful to make things easier between you.

Evening Look

Jasmine has a sparkling new outfit, and she wears it for a romantic evening. Help her find a matching shawl!

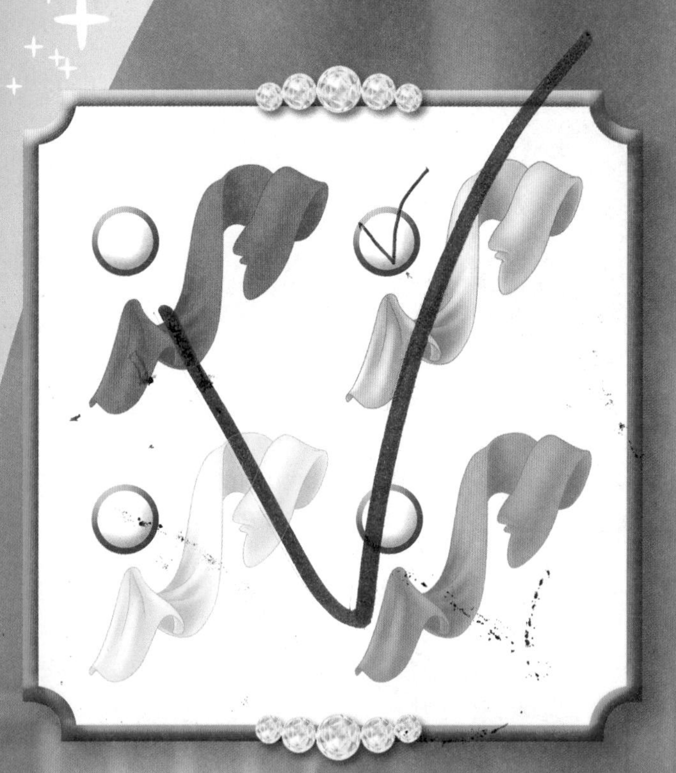

Jasmine sports turquoise gems! Some are oval, others are rhombus-shaped. Count them all!

Answers on page 173

A Ponytail for a Horseback Ride

Jasmine likes to be comfortable, especially on horseback, so she always rides with a long ponytail! Follow the four steps to make one like hers.

Connect the dots to discover the object Jasmine used before making her ponytail, then color it!

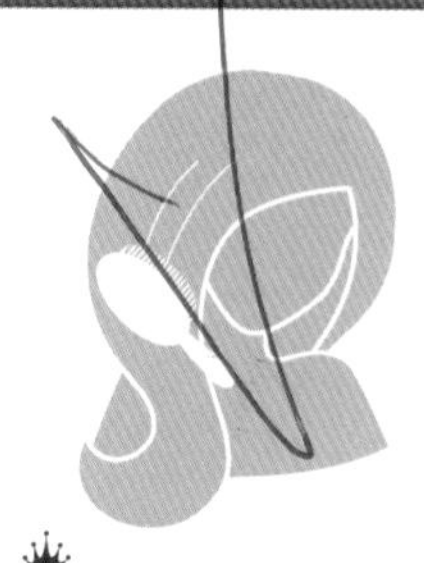

1. Brush your hair to eliminate all the knots.

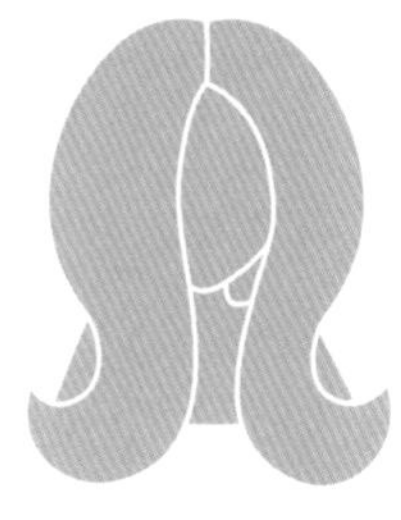

2. Use your hands to part your hair down the middle.

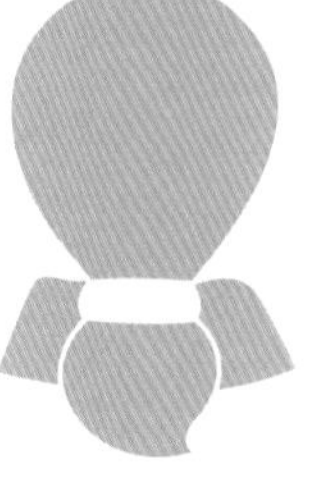

3. Tie your hair with an elastic band at shoulder height.

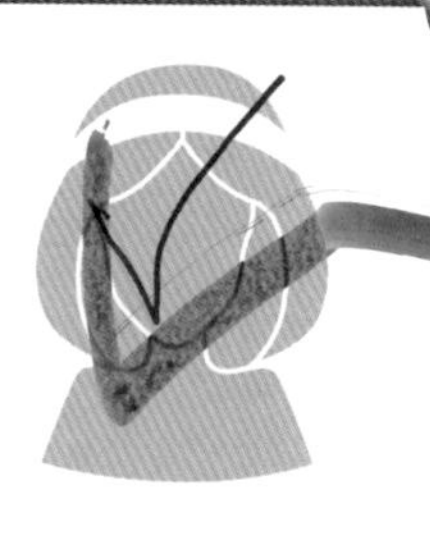

4. Put a colored ribbon around your head and tie it with a bow.

Answer on page 173

An Almost Romantic Date

OUCH!
AHEM . . . MAYBE **"CONFIDENT"** WASN'T EXACTLY THE RIGHT WORD!
COURAGE! IT'LL BE OK!
LET'S HOPE SO!
SOON . . .
WELL?!? **READY?**
FOR WHAT?

TO **FLY** ABOVE THE WINTER WOODS, OF COURSE!
GULP!

HOW ABOUT SOMETHING A LITTLE LESS **DANGEROUS**? LIKE WATCHING THE SNOWFLAKES . . .
DON'T WORRY! THIS OWL MAY BE A LITTLE **GREEN**, BUT IT'S GOT TALENT!

IF YOU SAY SO!

NEXT . . .
HOLD ON TIGHT!
POOR ME . . .
FLAP
FLAP

SEE? SMOOTH AS SILK!
WATCH OUT!

TOO LATE!
AAAAH!
BONK!
POFF!

OK, BACK THERE?!
ERR . . .

NOW CHECK THIS OUT!

MAYBE THINGS ARE WORKING OUT AFTER ALL . . .
FANTASTIC!
GLAD YOU LIKE IT!
MAYBE NOT . . .
AHHH! WHAT'S GOIN' ON?
I THINK OUR FRIEND HAS DECIDED TO LAND!
SWISSSSSSH
PLOP

HEE! HEE! THAT WAS GREAT!
YEAH . . . A TON OF FUN! SIGH . . .
POOR RO! A ROMANTIC DATE? IT WAS UPSETTING . . . TO SAY THE LEAST!

THE END

Magic Animals

Rare Species

Of the four images on the right, three are legendary creatures and one is a real animal. Match each creature with its correct description, then guess which one is the real animal.

A Dragon

B Loch Ness Monster

C Platypus

D Bigfoot

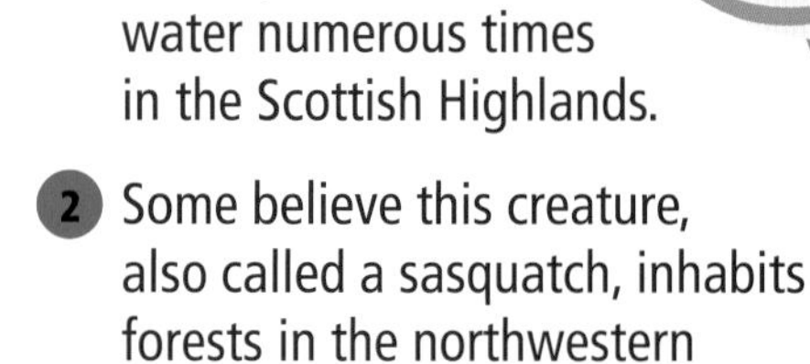

1. Legend has it that this famous monster has been spotted in the water numerous times in the Scottish Highlands.
2. Some believe this creature, also called a sasquatch, inhabits forests in the northwestern portion of North America.
3. Featured in myths among many cultures, this creature is often associated with wisdom and is commonly believed to possess magical powers.
4. Native to Australia, the strange appearance of this semiaquatic creature baffled scientists who first encountered it.

The real animal is:

Secret Creature

Color only the dotted spaces to reveal one of history's most beloved mythical creatures. Then, if you want, color the blank spaces a different color (or colors).

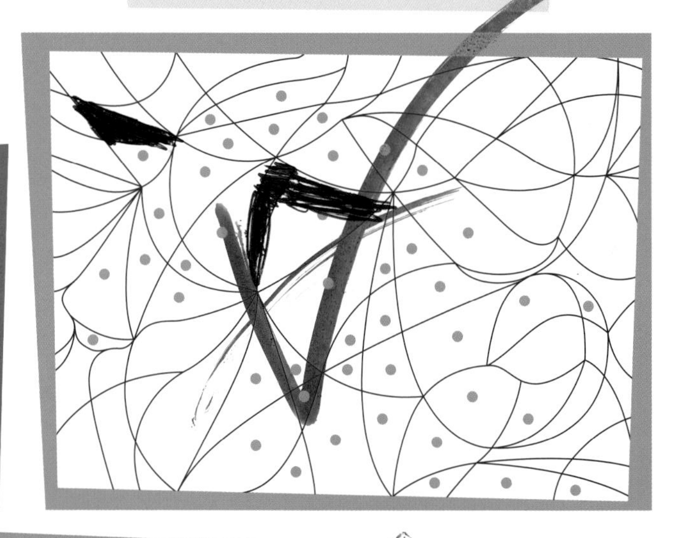

Answers on page 173

Rare Species

THE END

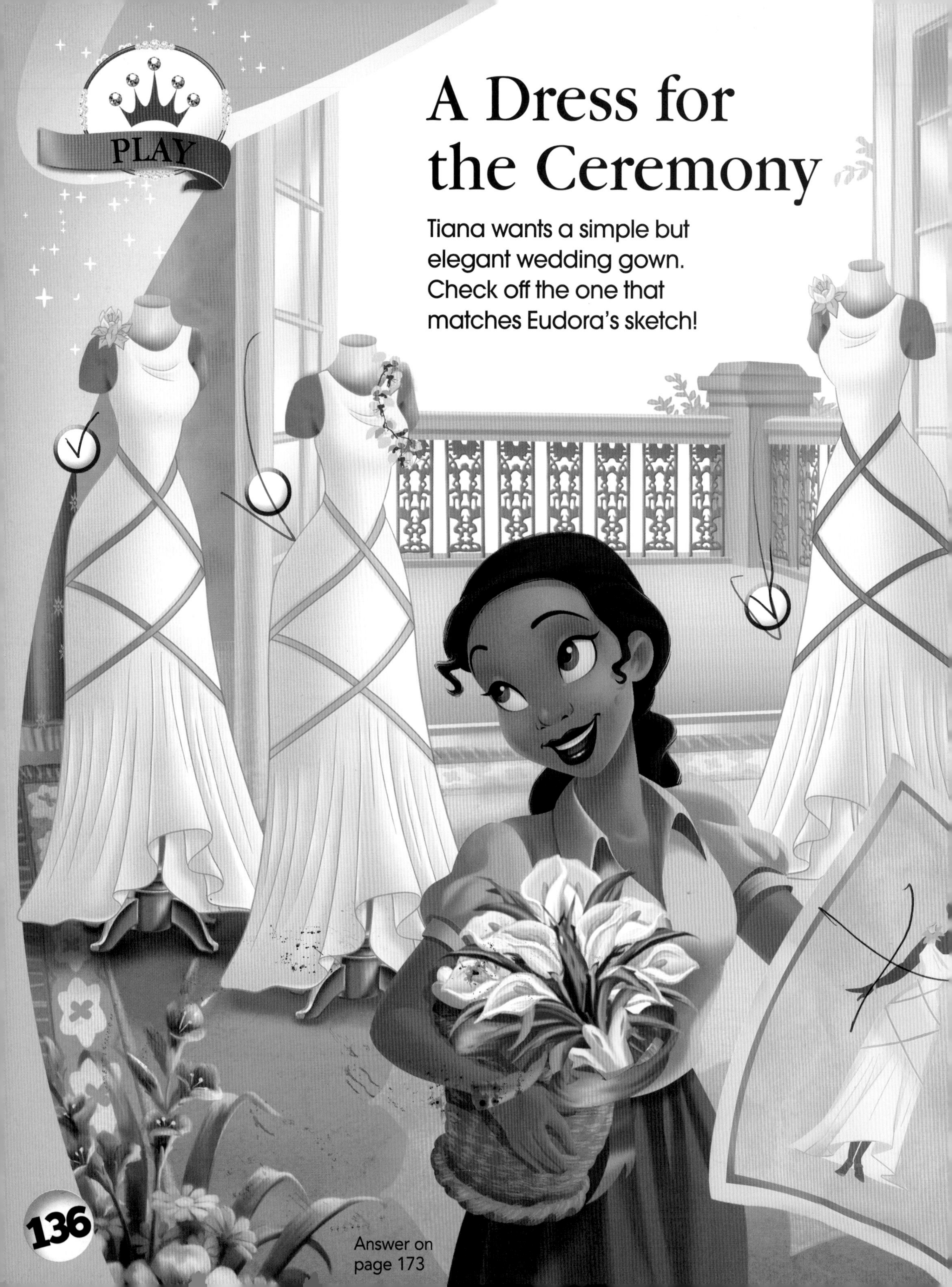

A Dress for the Ceremony

Tiana wants a simple but elegant wedding gown. Check off the one that matches Eudora's sketch!

Answer on page 173

Charlotte is putting the finishing touches on her dress. Check off the cloth decoration she has used.

Charlotte is still undecided about the color of the accessories she'll wear to Tiana's wedding. Give her a hand by putting the color groups together!

Answers on page 173

Bursting with Energy!

Dragonflies are some of the liveliest insects around! And it's no coincidence that one of them is Bluebell's partner in speedy flight.

A Bubbly Race!

One of the Pixie Hollow Games is Dragonfly Waterskiing.

Towed by dragonflies, the players skim the surface of the water while avoiding obstacles. The team that finishes with the best time wins!

Can you spot this dragonfly's missing detail? Tip: It's something important!

Answer on page 173

Amazing Wings in Action!

Dragonflies are among the world's fastest insects. They can accelerate and stop to hover, almost instantly, as well as move from side to side and up and down!

Their flight pattern changes all the time. Their wings flap up to 20 times a second, making them fast enough to be "invisible" to their prey!

A Long History . . .

Dragonflies live a double life. Their larvae—"babies"—are born in ponds, but as "grown-ups" they use their wings to fly out of the water at high speed!

They are insects with a long history behind them, with ancestors that date back some 300 million years—before the dinosaurs—and which were as big as seagulls!

Back to Nature

What if your dream job was connected to the great outdoors?

If you don't like the idea of staying in the same place indoors all day, **find a job that allows you to study nature and work outdoors!**

You might explore the world of plants as a botanist and work in a tropical forest or on a farm! There are thousands of careers related to the natural world.

Careers for Nature Lovers

Maybe you'd like to be a forest ranger and manage the land, plants, and animals in parks or wilderness areas. **Or, if you love the ocean, you could be a marine biologist** and study animals and plants that live in saltwater.

Which Job Is Your "Natural" Fit?

We've talked about three nature jobs on the next page. Find out which one works for you with this quiz!

1

You're most fascinated by:

- **A** Land animals
- **B** Ocean animals
- **C** Plant life

2

You would love to spend the day:

- **A** Hiking
- **B** Scuba diving
- **C** Planting a garden

3

Which of these bothers you the least?

- **A** Making sure others follow rules
- **B** Touching squishy things
- **C** Digging around in the dirt

4

You would like to live:

- **A** In a cabin in the mountains
- **B** On a boat in the tropics
- **C** In a farmhouse

5

You could also picture yourself working:

- **A** In law enforcement or fire prevention
- **B** At an aquarium or museum
- **C** At a nursery or landscaping business

Mostly **A**s:

FOREST RANGER

Hiking trails, wild animals, wilderness . . . sounds awesome to you!

Forest rangers might work in the desert, on mountains, or on a lake, overseeing a park, a game reserve, or historical site, for example.

Mostly **B**s:

MARINE BIOLOGIST

You love water and would enjoy studying and protecting sea life.

Marine biologists might spend time in labs, oceans, or salt marshes, working for industries, universities, aquariums, zoos, and other organizations.

Mostly **C**s:

BOTANIST

You'd like to learn more about plants as food, medicine —and beautiful things to look at!

Botanists work all over the world in all kinds of industries and in universities, botanical gardens, museums, environmental agencies, and more!

An Elegant Springtime Surprise

Cinderella was having a big party to celebrate the start of spring. "I want everything to be perfect," she told the Prince with glee.

She really enjoyed taking care of every detail. She began by planning a special menu with the royal chef. It included lots of tasty treats!

Along with the royal gardener, she made beautiful flower arrangements—she was thrilled! To finish things, she even chose lovely music for the dance.

But when the party was about to begin, not all the decorations had been set up. "My ladder is broken!" cried the assistant gardener. "We'll take care of the rest!" Jaq said.

5

Jaq, Gus, and the birds worked together quickly to put all the final decorations in place. Finally, everything was all set for the big event!

6

The only one missing was Cinderella, who had chosen a very unusual (for her) outfit for the occasion—sparkling pink! "Will the Prince like it?" she wondered.

7

Cinderella's royal garden party turned out to be a big success. She and the Prince danced for hours. "You're gorgeous in pink!" he told Cinderella.
"I wanted to surprise you with something unusual ... a very springtime color," Cinderella replied, smiling. And ~~they all~~ celebrated the arrival of the new season!

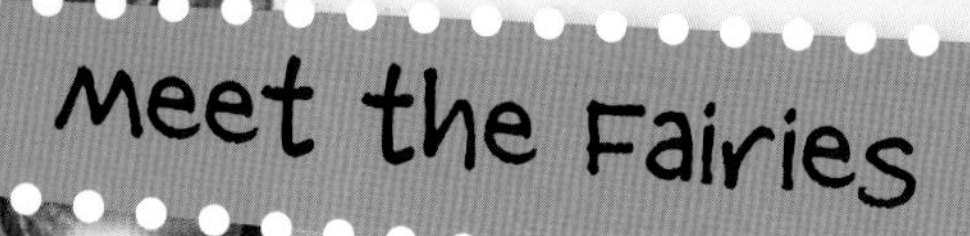

Bluebell

She's one of the peppiest garden fairies in Pixie Hollow!

Pure energy oozes from her every pore; her wings flutter as fast as those on the bumblebees in her garden! Her favorite flowers? Crocuses—because they're the first to bloom in spring and they grow quickly.

Bluebell is so excitable that her pals often ask her to slow down when she talks, otherwise they're not able to understand her! She likes to fly with Lester, a somewhat wayward dragonfly!

Flutter those wings and help Bluebell find the missing piece in this flowery scene!

1

2

3

Answer on page 173

What a Mess!

Clank and Bobble are gathering nuts and seeds to bring to Tinkers' Nook, but they've made such a mess! Help them by coloring in this scene.

Button Up!

Recycle buttons to make cool hair accessories! But first, find the button that matches your style.

START HERE

My favorite shoes are: 1

- A Cute dressy heels
- B Stylish riding boots
- C Funky retro wedges
- D Comfortable sandals

I'd describe myself as: 2

- A Feminine
- B Sophisticated
- C Bold
- D Down-to-earth

I most like to wear: 3

- A A frilly skirt
- B A crisp shirt
- C A jacket I decorated myself
- D Vintage jeans

I like to wear my hair: 4

- A In a fancy party updo
- B In a simple classic bun
- C With lots of colorful accents
- D Long, straight, and natural

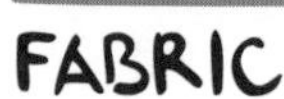

Mostly As:

FABRIC

The intricate designs on fabric buttons match your **feminine style**.

Mostly Bs:

METAL

You like **traditional looks**, and classic metal buttons are the perfect accent.

Mostly Cs:

PLASTIC

Plastic buttons **will add a bright jolt of color** to your bold wardrobe.

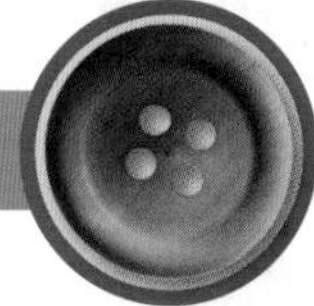

Mostly Ds:

WOOD

The warmth of wood complements your simple, **natural style.**

YOUR TURN!

Hair How-to

Glue one or more buttons to a plain hair clip to create a stylish accessory that's uniquely you!

Trip Tricks

World Traveler!

Figure out which vacation spot each of these postcards is from! Hawaii, France, or Japan? In the box below, choose two traditional fashion souvenirs to bring home from each destination and write the letter for each on the correct postcard.

Answers on page 173

A Stunning Kiss

Tiana's breathtaking story began when she kissed a frog! Look at this picture of the scene, then reconstruct the jumbled one on the right to match it.

1 2 3 4 5 6 7 8

Answers on page 173

Tinker Bell has
her hands full with
a real bookworm.
Color in this scene.

Sparking Wings
Pixie

Pick a Pattern

Which pattern fits in the blank space on the hoodie to complete the pattern?

Answer on page 173

Careers in Style

Where do you belong in the world of fashion?

There are thousands of fashion jobs out there! A few of them are shown below. Check the sentences that describe you best, then see which section has the most checks!

Check off one circle for each true statement.

Model

- I like to be the center of attention.
- I enjoy having my picture taken.
- I often practice different poses in the mirror.
- I love looking at fashion and celebrity magazines.
- I like trying on different outfits to see how they look.

You love fashion and celebrity, and you're aware of what makes you look your best. You might have what it takes to show off top designers' latest styles.

Stylist/Designer

- I like to experiment, putting together different outfits.
- I enjoy designing things with my hands.
- I like to draw.
- I wear different styles according to my mood.
- I always pay a lot of attention to what other people are wearing.

You have a keen interest in style and would be great at creating new fashions or putting together interesting looks for others.

Photographer

- I'm fascinated by interesting photos.
- I love art class.
- I enjoy observing people's actions and reactions.
- I tend to notice shadows, patterns, colors, and textures around me.
- I look for details when I'm taking a photo.

You have the technical interest and the artistic vision to make outfits look their best in cool magazines and videos.

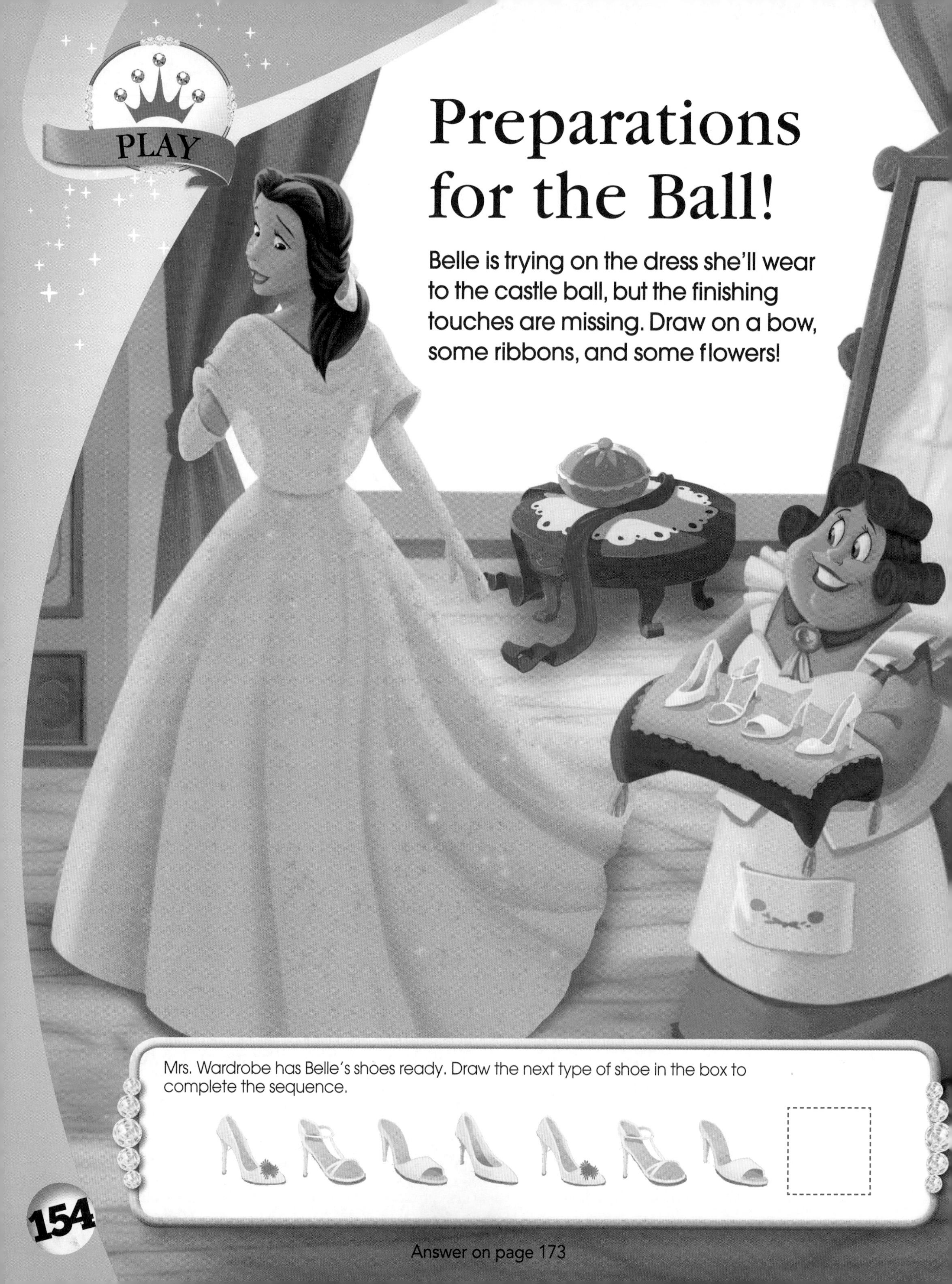

Preparations for the Ball!

Belle is trying on the dress she'll wear to the castle ball, but the finishing touches are missing. Draw on a bow, some ribbons, and some flowers!

Mrs. Wardrobe has Belle's shoes ready. Draw the next type of shoe in the box to complete the sequence.

Answer on page 173

Belle's really going to love this dress. Check off the objects that were used to make it.

Answer on page 173

Library Time!

Put your talent to the test and have a ball with your fairy friends!

Only the spines of these books can be seen from the shelves. Help the fairies match each one with its cover!

The correct matchups are:

a: ____________

b: ____________

c: ____________

d: ____________

e: ____________

Answers on page 173

Color this
picture of Tinker Bell
in the library!

Message in the Mirror

What a lovely mirror shimmering inside the Dwarfs' comfy cottage—it's a gift for Snow White. Connect the dots to see what is in the mirror.

Answer on page 173

A Royal Birthday Party

Rapunzel will soon celebrate her birthday and she wants to be sure her look is perfect! Check off the image she sees in the mirror.

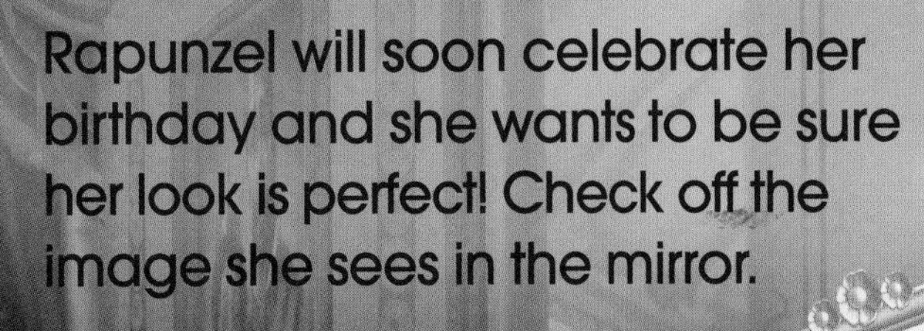

You're invited to Rapunzel's birthday party, too! What to wear? Complete and color this dress any way you like!

Answer on page 173

Let's Work!

Help your Fairy friends solve these riddles!

In Tinkers' Nook there's always something to do! Complete the scene by drawing lines to match up the missing pieces with the spaces they belong in.

A

B

C

Answers on page 173

Fun Under the Stars!

There are five differences in the bottom picture. Can you spot and circle them all?

Answers on page 173

Are You More Like Minnie or Daisy?

Find out which character matches your personality with this quiz!

Start Here!

Some of your greatest strengths are:

- A Imagination and ability to solve problems
- B Persistence and dedication

2 **Your friends think you are:**

- A Devoted
- B Dynamic

3 **At the beach, you like to:**

- A Sit under an umbrella and chat or read
- B Surf or swim

4 **Your favorite hobby is:**

- A Designing clothes.
- B Playing sports

5 **Your must-have accessory is:**

- A Your barrette
- B Your sneakers

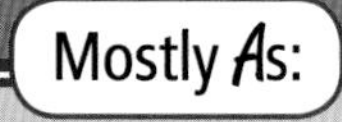

MINNIE

Cheerful, can-do Minnie is your perfect match! You can find a creative answer to any problem, and you're the glue that holds your crew together!

Mostly Bs:

DAISY

You have a lot in common with loyal, energetic Daisy! You love being active, and you fearlessly plunge into new challenges!

Fashion Passion

YEAH! THEY'RE LOOKING FOR TRENDY GIRLS TO PUT ON THEIR COVER!
WHICH IS WHY THEIR PHOTOGRAPHERS ARE GOING TO BE HERE TOMORROW!
WOW! WE'VE JUST GOT TO GET THAT HAT!
HA! HA! HA!
YOU GUYS DON'T EVEN KNOW WHERE TO LOOK FOR THAT HAT! YOU'LL NEVER FIND IT!
NEVER . . .
. . . EVER!
BUT MY MOM'S FAMOUS AND THANKS TO HER CONNECTIONS, I WILL!
!
SHE . . .
. . .WILL!
THE COVER OF STAR GIRL IS ALL MINE!
!
HA! HA!
HA! HA!
WHAT NERVE!
ESPELLALMONL!
?
I'D BETTER NOT TRANSLATE!
WE'VE GOT TO FIND THAT HAT!
WE CAN'T LET ABIGAIL END UP ON THE COVER!
MEET ME AFTER SCHOOL! I KNOW WHERE TO FIND IT!

BUT . . .
LADY WHO?
LADY DADA, THE SINGER!
HOW CAN YOU NOT KNOW WHO SHE IS?

THIS IS THE TRENDIEST SHOP IN TOWN! I WAS SURE WE'D FIND IT HERE!
IT DOESN'T MATTER, MACY!
KONNIE, ANYTHING ONLINE?
NOTHING! IT'S NOT FOR SALE!

MAYBE ABIGAIL WAS RIGHT! WE'LL NEVER FIND IT!
BUT THEN AGAIN . . .

. . . WE CAN COME UP WITH ANOTHER SOLUTION!
WITH YOUR SKILLS AND SOME COOL FABRIC, WE CAN MAKE ONE OURSELVES!
YOU'RE RIGHT!
IT'LL TURN OUT GREAT!

BUT . . .
UM . . .

PFFT!

UM . . .

I GIVE UP!
HMM . . .

HEY, THIS MIGHT NOT BE LADY DADA'S HAT, BUT IF IT WAS A PURSE . . .
?

MINNIE, THIS BOW WOULD LOOK PERFECT ON YOU!
AND THIS? SHOULD WE USE IT AS A NECKLACE?

HA! HA! HA! GUYS, YOU'RE FANTASTIC! JUST LET ME PUT THE FINISHING TOUCHES ON THEM!
GIRLFRIENDS ARE MADE TO CHEER EACH OTHER UP!

AND SO . . .
PERFECT! WE MIGHT NOT END UP BEING THE COVER GIRLS, BUT NOBODY HAS ACCESSORIES LIKE OURS!

LOOK AT ALL THE PEOPLE!
HEY, THERE'S TOM! HE'S TAKING THE PHOTOGRAPHERS SOMETHING TO DRINK!

HERE I AM! YOUR COVER GIRL HAS ARRIVED!

HUH?

AAAARGH!
SPLOSH
LOOK AT WHAT YOU'VE DONE!
SORRY, ABIGAIL, BUT YOU SCARED ME! WHAT'S ON YOUR HEAD ANYWAY, A MONSTER?

YOU DON'T KNOW THE FIRST THING ABOUT FASHION!
HA! HA! HA!
HA! HA! HA! IF YOU WANTED TO GET PEOPLE'S ATTENTION, YOU GOT IT!

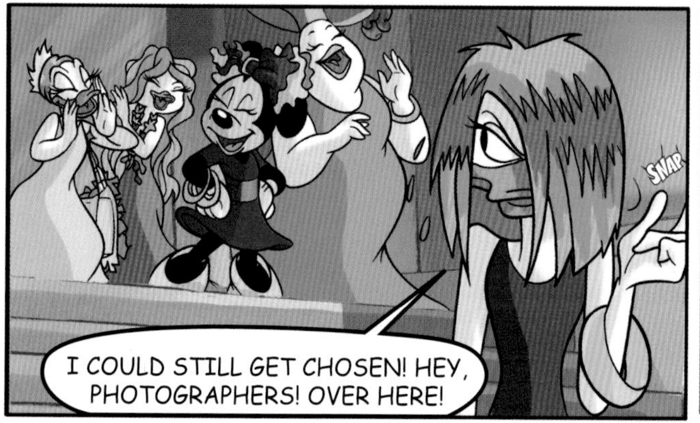
SNAP
I COULD STILL GET CHOSEN! HEY, PHOTOGRAPHERS! OVER HERE!

WOW, SEE THAT?
WHAT A LOOK!
WHAT STYLE!

AW, YOU'RE TOO KIND! YOU'RE MAKING ME BLUSH . . .
YOUR ACCESSORIES ARE JUST GORGEOUS!

CLICK
AND THEY'RE ALL HANDMADE!
!

YOU GIRLS ARE PERFECT FOR OUR COVER!
CHEEESE!
FLASH
CLICK
FLASH

The End

Great Shot!

Grab your BFF and a camera, and get ready for a photo-tastic good time!

Do you like taking pictures? Or maybe posing? You and your BFF can take turns doing each and learn a lot about photography—plus have fun, of course!

Getting Started

First, make sure you and your BFF are familiar with the camera you're using. Check where the focus, zoom, and other features are located. Then choose a good spot: a blank wall, a field of flowers—whatever would make a nice backdrop. Now follow the tips on this page to take perfect pics!

Made to Model

Looking good in a photo is just a matter of knowing a few basic posing tips:

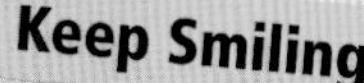

Practice a natural smile. Don't clench your teeth; try to relax your lips.

Full Tilt

Faces look better when shot from a slight angle. And try some creative expressions!

Add Something

Using your hands in different poses can bring even more attention to your face.

Open Up!

Avoid blinks: Close your eyes, have the photographer count down, and open just before the click!

Royal Details

Aurora is preparing to welcome important guests to the palace. Spot the five differences between these two scenes! Put a check at the bottom of the page for each one you find.

Now all Aurora needs is a rose to give to each lady in attendance. Look at the flower above and find the one that matches!

Answers on page 173

PAGE 7

COURAGE

PAGE 17

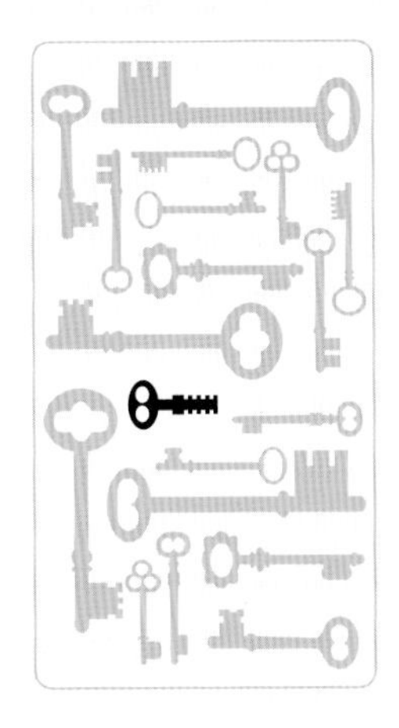

PAGE 20

There are 14 fireflies

PAGE 23

The shape is a heart

O	B	G	T	O	E	L	A	I
V	P	A	L	Z	D	U	B	G
P	A	I	R	F	A	L	L	Y
I	T	S	U	R	T	G	O	E
H	A	P	P	I	N	E	S	S
D	J	O	Y	E	V	O	L	E
N	Y	F	U	N	N	Y	T	U
I	H	U	D	D	A	F	V	R
U	O	I	J	S	M	T	A	L
R	H	M	I	Q	K	L	S	I

PAGE 24

PAGE 25

PAGES 26-27

MINISTER OF SPRING—5 AND 6
MINISTER OF WINTER—2 AND 8
MINISTER OF SUMMER—1 AND 4
MINISTER OF AUTUMN—3 AND 7

PAGE 28

PAGE 29

A. 2 and 8
B. 3 and 5
C. 4 and 7
D. 1 and 6

PAGE 31

PAGE 32

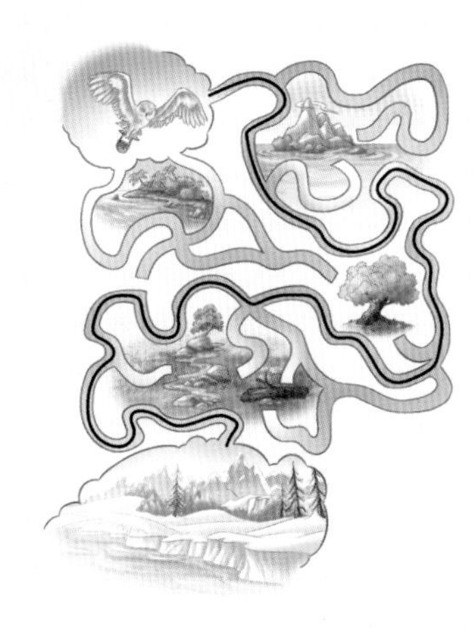

PAGE 33

PAGE 43

B

PAGE 48

2

PAGE 49

B is the correct shadow

PAGE 51

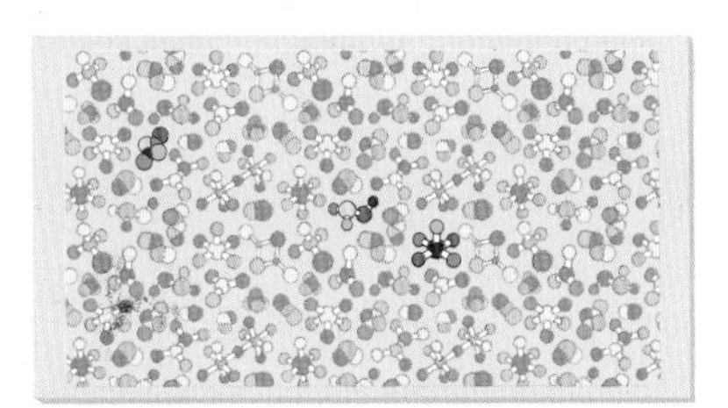

PAGES 52-53

A baby dog is called a puppy.

PAGES 58-59

PAGE 60

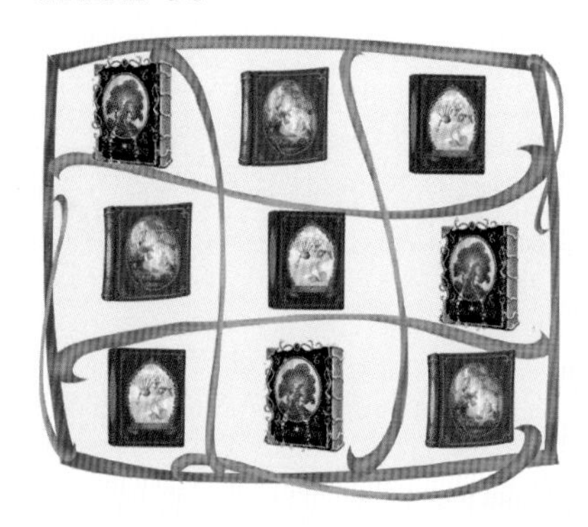

PAGE 62

PAGE 71

B

PAGES 72-73

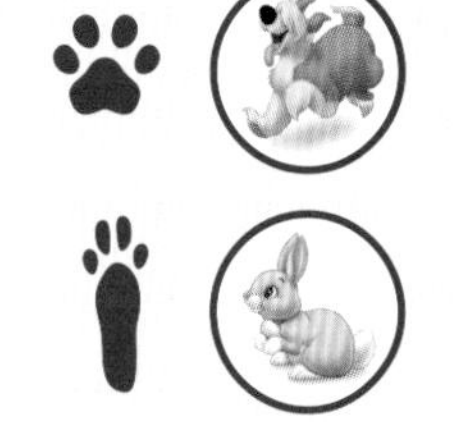

PAGE 75

1

PAGE 81

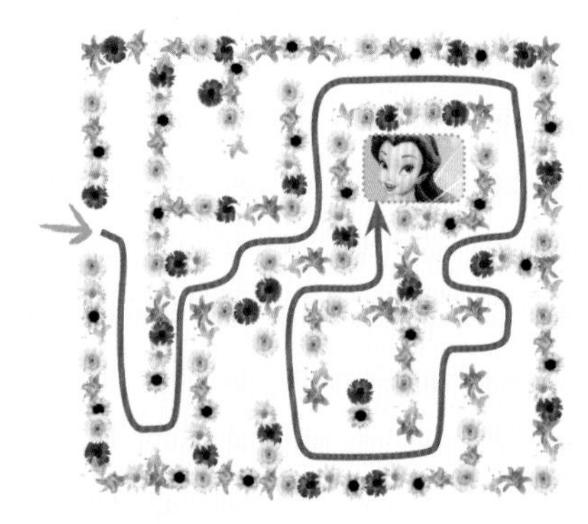

PAGE 82

Macy: 4, 8, B, D
Minnie: 5, 7, E, H
Leonard: 1, 6, A, F
Daisy: 2, 3, C, G

PAGE 83

Italy—4
U.S.A.—1
India—2
Japan—3

Four-leaf clover search—3

PAGE 84

PAGE 85

PAGES 90-91

It's an octopus

PAGE 93

Tink has used:
basket (2)
comb (3)
twigs (4)
funnel (8)

PAGE 96

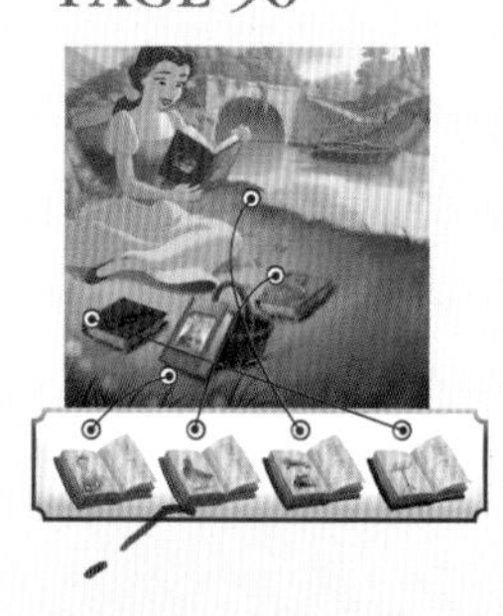

PAGE 97

PAGE 98

The last two flowers

PAGE 99

PIXIE DUST

Shadow number 2

PAGES 106-107

PAGE 111

A—2, B—5, C—6, D—1, E—3, F—4

PAGE 112

A—False (The idea is credited to American environmentalist Gaylord Nelson.)

B—False (Scientists aren't sure, but estimate it could be 500-1,000 years.)

C—True!

PAGES 114-115

PAGE 117

The Keeper

PAGE 118

The correct sequence is:
d, a, c, b, f, e

PAGE 119

Connect the dots—butterfly

5 blueberries, 3 raspberries, 1 bunch of grapes, 2 blueberry muffins, 1 cherry tart, 4 strawberries, 2 sesame buns

PAGE 121

A: 1 and 6
B: 2 and 4
C: 3 and 5

PAGE 122-123

Tiana and Cinderella have updos.

PAGE 128

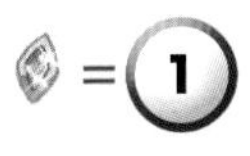

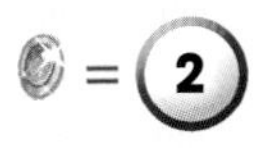

PAGE 129

Hairbrush

PAGE 134

Rare Species:
A—3, B—1, C—4, D—2
Real animal: Platypus
Secret Creature: Unicorn

PAGE 136

PAGE 137

PAGE 138

Its wings are missing

PAGE 144

The missing piece is number 2

PAGE 147

Postcard 1: France—A and D
Postcard 2: Japan—B and F
Postcard 3: Hawaii—C and E

PAGES 148-149

PAGE 152

Pattern d

PAGE 154

PAGE 155

PAGE 156

a—2, b—4, c—3, d—5, e—1

PAGE 158

It's a heart

PAGE 159

PAGE 160

1—D, 2—C, 3—B, 4—A

PAGE 161

1. Tink's hair bun is missing
2. One firefly is missing an antenna
3. Iridessa is missing a wing
4. Iridessa's skirt has an extra petal
5. The light container has two branches

PAGE 170